THE LAST AIR FORCE ONE

A POST-APOCALYPTIC SAGA

JEFF KIRKHAM
JASON ROSS

AIR FORCE ONE

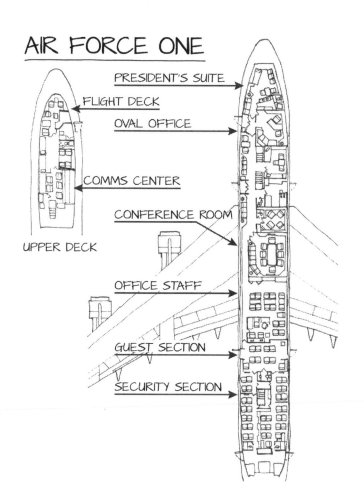

PRESIDENT'S SUITE

FLIGHT DECK

OVAL OFFICE

COMMS CENTER

CONFERENCE ROOM

OFFICE STAFF

GUEST SECTION

SECURITY SECTION

UPPER DECK

1

A nuclear blast looked nothing like a mushroom cloud from so close.

Dutch's mind struggled to find solid ground. The same thing had happened on September 11th, 2001 when he watched an airliner hurl into the twin towers on TV. Just like that morning twenty years ago, President Nathaniel "Dutch" McAdams' mouth hung agape and his knees went to water as he watched America being incinerated by its enemies.

The picture on the television jerked side-to-side. The iPhone cameraman must have been running away from the blast while filming toward it. A massive sphere of light wrapped around a cluster of high-rise office buildings. The light overwhelmed the tiny camera and the buildings vanished in a starburst. A split-second later, the light receded, and the camera adjusted to the exposure, the buildings still standing.

The President of the United States exhaled. He had been holding his breath for the last twenty seconds. Returning to this terrible reality, he watched as one of the wealthiest cities in America crouched before a thunderclap of flame.

The windows of the office buildings vaporized as the over-pressure of the blast pulsed through the high-rise, sucking atomized glass and a hundred thousand pieces of paper into thin air. Dutch watched for falling bodies but saw only ticker tape floating leisurely toward earth.

He already knew that the shockwave wouldn't be followed by white-hot flame—otherwise, the cameraman wouldn't have uploaded the video to the internet. If the man had burned up, the president and his staff wouldn't be watching him run for his life on the big screen TV in the Oval Office. Apparently, the explosion wasn't enough to incinerate all of downtown Los Angeles. Still, the ground in L.A. must've heaved like a kicking mule. With the cameraman running pell-mell, it was hard to tell.

The cameraman slowed, either from over-exertion or from the realization that the fireball wasn't going to immolate him. A heavy-set man with a wispy beard turned the camera on himself, gasping for air and stating the obvious.

"Los Angeles has been hit by a nuclear weapon. I'm going to post this on Instagram and run for my car. I don't know how long I have before the fallout gets me. I want my family to know I love them. Goodbye."

The TV flipped back to a blond-haired man in a suit, sitting behind a desk at a Fox News studio, probably in New York City. The newscaster began to repeat what everyone who had watched the last fifteen seconds already knew: Los Angeles had been attacked.

Dutch blinked away his amazement and resumed his role as the most powerful man on Earth.

"What else do we know?" he asked his team assembled in his office. They had been working almost non-stop for two days on a financial crisis that had already been threatening to swamp the world economy, even prior to the nuke. This latest attack—and it could only be an attack—raised a thousand questions. Who was aggressing against the United States, and what did it have to do with the dirty bomb in Saudi Arabia and the crash of the stock market? The string of events made absolutely no sense to McAdams.

Nobody from the president's team spoke, the newscaster droning in the background, repeating essentially the same sentence over-and-over.

The doors to the Oval Office burst inward and Dutch's contingent of secret service agents fanned out in the room, peering at his staff with unnecessary suspicion.

"Mister President, we're taking you to Air Force One right now."

Dutch had argued with his protective detail before and he'd always lost. Whatever power he held as president didn't extend to bending the will of the government organizations he supposedly commanded. Secret Service policy, as with all governmental agencies, spanned many dozen presidents. There was only so much he could do to alter the institutional will of the over four hundred agencies, sub-agencies and departments, many with more than two hundred years of bureaucratic inertia. Most days Dutch felt like a conductor standing in front of an orchestra, the musicians with bags over their heads.

He grabbed his laptop and cellphone before his security dragged him away.

"Janice, get Sam Greaney and Zach Jackson to meet me at Andrews AFB. They need to be on that plane." He turned to the secret service agent holding his arm. "Where's my family?"

"In a helo on their way to Andrews, sir."

"Thank you... Robbie, come with us."

Robbie Leforth, Dutch's chief of staff looked rattled. The younger man jumped up from the sofa and blundered toward the phalanx of secret service agents now heading out the door.

"Robbie. You're going to need your laptop," the President

pointed toward the coffee table as he was being pulled from his office and into the hallway.

2

U pon boarding Air Force One, Dutch broke ranks with his protective detail and headed back into the section of the plane set aside for reporters and his office staff. He needed to check on his family.

His wife, Sharon, his twenty-three-year-old daughter, Abigail and his twenty-year-old son, Teddy were buckled in, ready for the Boeing 747-8 to get in the air.

Dutch noticed a cluster of three special forces operators in full military kit, speaking privately with Secretary of Defense Sam Greaney. He overheard something about "a full frange load-out" which meant nothing to Dutch. His secret servicemen stood in a separate cluster, eyeballing the other gunmen. Nothing about the scene alarmed the president. Greaney's personal security detail were Army Delta Force, and his own secret service detail distrusted everyone as a general rule.

After trading a quick touch-of-the-hand with his wife, and a smile with each of his now-adult children, Dutch strode with purpose toward the front of the gleaming aircraft.

The glamor of Air Force One still hadn't worn off on Dutch. Aside from the top-secret features of the plane, no effort had

been spared for style and comfort. Even the office, guest, security and press sections in the back of the hulking fuselage put
most first-class sections to shame; with wide leather seats—each
with an array of connection and entertainment options
imbedded in their consoles. On every bulkhead, crystalline LCD
screens silently scrolled through passenger safety instructions
produced exclusively for the president's personal jumbo jet.

Heading toward the nose of the plane, the duties of
governing the greatest empire the world had ever seen took
precedence over design. The main hallway dog-legged to the
port side of the plane, affording space for a large conference and
dining room, a senior staff office, the plane's galley, a small
medical office and the Oval Office. The president and first lady's
executive suite filled the nose of the aircraft, where one might
expect the pilots.

The Boeing 747, one of the first "jumbo jets," not only ran
much wider than most jets, but offered an upper deck in the
front of the craft, where Air Force One housed a state-of-the-art
communications center and the flight cockpit.

Everything about Air Force One, from its fit and finish to its
capability to stay aloft indefinitely through mid-air refueling,
spoke to the incomprehensible might of the United States of
America. Stepping aboard the aircraft was like walking into the
throne rooms of medieval Europe. Allies and rivals alike were to
take notice: the U.S.A. ruled the Earth.

Whereas the Oval Office in the White House had been
packed with economic and diplomatic advisors, the front section
of Air Force One bristled with military men. Secretary of
Defense Sam Greaney sat on Dutch's couch and uniformed
servicemen hustled past on their way to the communications
center on the second floor of the aircraft.

The use of nuclear weapons would typically have that effect,
Dutch reasoned. Still, even as a Republican, he had developed

the habit of leaning away when the war hawks appeared. Almost from day one as president, Dutch found himself choking back on the military, as though it were a pit bull straining on its leash.

It made Dutch think of one of his father's favorite truisms: *to a hammer, everything's a nail.*

"I would love an update," President Dutch McAdams requested as he settled behind his desk. The plane hadn't taken to the air yet, but he had just spent twenty-five minutes in a helicopter without any news.

SecDef Sam Greaney would have the latest information, given that the military undoubtedly had aircraft circling over Los Angeles and maybe even troops on the ground by now. The secretary of defense would probably become Dutch's best source for hard data from this point forward, no matter how much Dutch would've preferred to use domestic resources.

"Mister President, F-35s out of Miramar are currently overflying Los Angeles harbor, and we have zero indication of a follow-on threat as of this time," Sam reported. "Uncorroborated initial sit reps indicate that the device detonated four kilometers out to sea and that damage to Los Angeles proper was collateral overpressure and not the primary detonation."

Dutch understood the words, but Sam Greaney had gotten into the habit of over-using military jargon since his posting to secretary of defense. Sam had served briefly as an Air Force officer three decades back, primarily working in intelligence and then working for the CIA. After that, he had moved into the private sector. Dutch had hoped that over twenty years in business would have made Sam a bridge between the military and civilian worlds, but during the last two years as SecDef, Sam had become something of a "fan boy" of the generals, officers and special forces soldiers that reported to him as secretary of defense. Perhaps Sam's time in the military hadn't been enough to answer that burning question inside most men: am I a warrior or am I not?

"Thank you, Sam. Could you please say that again, maybe in a way we're all sure to understand?"

Sam Greaney blinked back the veiled criticism and ran his hands through his cropped gray hair as he gathered his thoughts. He tucked his dress shirt into his belt, tidying up the fabric around his trim waist. In the last two years, he had picked up the military officer habit of maintaining his fitness, despite being over sixty-years-old.

"Well, in civilian terms, I would say that the bomb seems to have been a small one. Maybe even a backpack nuke. We have no idea why, but it exploded three miles offshore from Los Angeles. We're still trying to figure out why it didn't hit L.A. directly. We have hearsay reports of L.A.P.D. intercepting a small sea craft right before detonation. There are no hostile warships in the area, and we have no reason to believe that enemy forces are in theater. But it's hard to say for sure because from the sky, L.A. appears to be in total chaos."

The airplane rumbled as it taxied on the runway, causing a short a pause in the briefing.

"Chaos?" Zach Jackson asked. As per Dutch's request, both his SecDef and attorney general had made it onto the plane in time for takeoff.

Dutch had the same question: how had the bomb affected the rioting that was already going on in southern California. Los Angeles had been in a crisis even before the nuclear attack. More accurately, Orange County, California had been experiencing blackouts and brownouts over the previous two days, and the power problems had spread to the margins of L.A. as had rioting and civil disorder.

Dutch had never been entirely clear on the difference between Los Angeles and Orange County. They both seemed to be part of the same, sprawling mass of strip malls, commercial buildings and tract homes, stretching from Camp Pendleton in the south to Ventura in the north. Orange County had been experiencing rioting as had some parts of Los Angeles due to several days of power outages. Dutch and his staff were just working on a federal response to the rioting when they were interrupted by news of the nuclear attack.

Like Zach Johnson, the president wanted to know if the attack had stopped the rioting. They were both probably thinking of 9/11, when America quickly unified in the face of an attack on one of their great cities.

"Well," Sam Greaney explained, "We're talking about F-35 pilots looking down from several thousand feet going point-seven-five mach. It's not like they can see the expression on peoples' faces. They're telling us that a mass exodus is under-way, worse than before, if that's even possible. I have troops rolling from El Segundo to give us eyes on the ground. I expect a report any minute." He looked down, pulling his cell phone from his pocket and thumbing the screen, scrolling through messages, probably looking for a report from L.A..

"Is that a report from L.A., Sam?" the President prodded the secretary of defense, who had become engrossed in something on his cell phone. "Yes sir. Sorry, sir. I'm trying to find out more." Sam Greaney sat down on the couch between Robbie Leforth, Chief of Staff, and Janice Brown, the president's personal secretary.

"I'll let you know more when I know more," Sam Greaney said before getting lost in the data stream.

3

Everyone had been cleared out of the Oval Office by the flight attendant for takeoff. The president could buckle into his office chair, but everyone else had to take their assigned seats until they reached cruising altitude.

Dutch pondered the irony of the moment. California might be spiraling out of control, caught in a grab bag of disasters, but the pinnacle decision-makers, upon whom millions of people relied for leadership, were being herded to their seats by a flight attendant just to make absolutely sure nobody bumped their head during takeoff.

Dutch smiled despite the tension grinding in his gut. How had the world come to this: diminutive safety concerns and ponderous policy outweighing common sense? Nine-tenths of the straightforward actions he wanted to take as president had been stymied by political exigency, social sensitivity, and good, old fashioned inertia. Doing the smart thing had never been more difficult in politics, even with mind-boggling technology at their fingertips.

For the thousandth time, he compared his presidency to Abraham Lincoln's. Oh how Dutch would've loved to lead the country back when a president could turn the rudder and the ship would follow.

He closed his eyes and tried to make sense of the deluge of information he faced since waking up that morning. What had started out as a terrorist attack in the Middle East had become an energy crisis which had transformed into a stock market problem. Then a bomb exploded off the California coast. Dutch failed to grasp the connection. It felt like a tangle of string and he couldn't find the end.

This happened a lot as POTUS. He faced so many data points, factors and question marks that it became impossible to get them all on the same map inside his head. Having done this job for two years now, Dutch had a lot more sympathy for the guy he replaced. Doing the "smart thing," even with more information than anyone on the planet, still involved a ton of guesswork.

He sat back in his chair and inventoried the events of the last few days, stripping them of drama as best he could.

Unless his people had missed something, the first big dollop of trouble had been the dirty bomb hitting the oil transfer station in Saudi Arabia three days before. The CIA's best guess was that Iran mounted the nuke attack, for some reason that only made sense to that maniac, religious dictator who ran their country. Putting the *whys* and *wherefores* aside, the bomb in Saudi Arabia had generated a stampede in the energy markets.

The U.S. had been a net exporter of energy for some time, but the commodity pricing of oil still rocked and rolled based on global factors. How much oil was coming out of Siberia? What craziness was going on in the minds of OPEC? How were the Arabs, Jews and Iranians behaving this week?

American gas on the American mainland was secure. But the American commodities market was not secure at all.

Rising tides lift all boats, as the saying went. But plunging tides also dumped all boats in the mud. With the price of oil skyrocketing, the first boat to hit the seafloor had been the Union Pacific Railroad.

The venerable, old railroad's sickly stock had been propped up for years by cheap diesel fuel and the coal transport market. But coal had become a swearword for the eco-minded denizens of America. Coal transport, from mines to power plants, meant a hell of a lot to Union Pacific Railroad and their shareholders. When diesel fuel doubled in price, the railroad stock fell off a cliff, and their fuel contracts hit stop-losses, giving the fuel suppliers a chance to renege on their deals. The ensuing contractual stutter-step temporarily halted all rail movement in the western United States, which meant that coal couldn't get where it needed to go. No matter how much the eco-social-justice crowd hated coal, the dirty fossil fuel still provided thirty percent of the power for their electric cars and cappuccino makers. Like a family with an awkward, homeless uncle, America couldn't just abandon coal without first figuring out a sensible game plan. But, the collapse of the energy market had rendered these questions moot. Union Pacific and the coal it shipped had taken a premature dirt nap, and Dutch had no idea how a president was supposed to fix things when markets convulsed entirely on their own.

On the opposite side of the political divide from the eco-minded, the ultra-right citizen militias had been on edge lately. While they generally liked Dutch as president, the militia types couldn't stand the federal government. The week prior, there had been an unfortunate shooting between a militia group in Texas and a federal park ranger. Five men had died. On top of that, the dirty bomb attack in the Middle East had the alt-right screaming "false flag operation" though it wasn't clear who they thought had secretly orchestrated the bombing. For all Dutch knew, they could be right. He'd seen stranger things in his time in politics.

As fate would have it, the biggest power plant supplying Orange County and the eastern third of Los Angeles County sat on a hotbed of militia activity: the town of Delta, Utah—one of the same power plants that missed their coal shipment because Union Pacific Railroad lost its diesel supplier. The Delta, Utah power plant was hundreds of miles from Los Angeles. But losing that chunk of electricity during the end of summer in sweltering Los Angeles basin had an impact nobody might've imagined.

When air conditioners ground to a halt in Orange County and L.A., on top of the problems with the stock market, some urban Californians took to the streets looting and rioting, with social media accelerating the civil unrest into another iteration of the L.A. riots.

At that juncture, the details got fuzzy for Dutch, which was a sure sign that someone in the chain of bureaucracy had been obfuscating his information. Dutch's money was on the latest loud-mouthed, Hollywood actor-slash-governor of California. He and Dutch hadn't seen eye-to-eye, even though the President was raised in rural California before being swept away by the Ivy League scene on the East Coast. The President had grown up in the tiny mountain town of Bishop, California, a far cry from the metropolitan scramble of Oakland, where the California governor went to high school.

Somehow, in a heavy-handed attempt to make sure that the coal supply was restored to the power plant in Utah, the Governor of the State of California sent National Guard vehicles into a neighboring state to see that the coal arrived.

By some perverse stroke of luck or genius, the militia group in Delta captured the California National Guard's advance force and blockaded the town. Dutch didn't know if anyone had died in the conflict, but he knew that once the Delta Desert Patriots pointed guns at American servicemen, there had been no turning back for the little town and its erstwhile patriots. As far as Dutch knew, the town and the power plant were still locked down by camouflaged radicals.

This morning—which seemed like yesterday to Dutch—there had been so much crisis on his desk that he hadn't had time to address the militia group seizing control of a town and a power plant. Before he could get to it, someone rushed into the Oval Office and turned on Fox News, where Dutch and his staff witnessed the first nuclear weapon ever used against the United States of America.

Dutch could follow the bouncing ball from the Saudi Arabian attack, to the failure of Union Pacific Railroad, to the shutdown of the power plant. He could even see how the destruction of a major oil pumping station and tanker loading facility in the Middle East could cause the stock market to hiccup. Many corporations had been flying high for years on cheap gas. Expensive gas would hit a lot of stock prices.

But how did a small militia in a tiny town in Utah come to play such a pivotal role in escalating civil disorder in Southern California? What the hell did any of this have to do with the nuclear attack in L.A.? Could the Iranians have mounted the nuke attack in L.A. as a follow up to the Saudi nuke? Why would one be a dirty bomb and the other be a fission bomb? And why would the bombs be three days apart?

Now in his mid-sixties, President Dutch McAdams had seen his share of weird chains of events. *Life is long and strange,* he liked to say. Not every puzzle piece fit into a puzzle. Random chance resulted in peculiar, sometimes spooky combinations, like the triggers that started World War One or even the financial collapse of 2008; *Black Swan Events,* as economists liked to call them.

People imagined that random chance played out more

evenly than it actually did. While flipping "tails" ten times in a row was unlikely, in practice, it happened surprisingly often. Human history flipped tails ten times in a row with regularity, and then mankind paid the price with interest.

There might be no connection whatsoever between the two nuclear devices. Or it might be a nefarious plot. Or it all might be a series of hapless accidents. Dutch might find the link tomorrow or he might never find it. Even the president wasn't omniscient, he knew all too well.

But Dutch had been elected by the people of America to diagnose problems and fix them, and he would be damned if he wouldn't do exactly that.

4

Dutch awoke at 5 a.m. on Air Force One, his cell phone vibrating, overfull with an alarming stream of text messages.

After hours of pawing through unsatisfying slivers of news, he and Sharon had finally called it a night. They continued their three thousand mile circuit over America that would keep them away from the coast, where an enemy submarine could conceivably shoot them out of the sky. As soon as the military had more solid answers on the attack, they would return home to Andrews Air Force Base and Washington D.C.. The glamor of the airplane had already worn off and Dutch yearned to be on the ground.

To his knowledge, they had never done this before—moving a president to "WarFlight Status" during a heightened threat. President Bush had spent only three hours in the air after the 9/11 attacks, and that had been to get him from a grade school in Georgia to Strategic Air Command in Omaha, Nebraska.

Dutch lifted his window shade and looked out into the still-dark morning sky, the slight orange scrim of dawn etching a line to the east of their flight path. Two red lights blinked in the distance, probably the E-4B Nightwatch that served as a flying command center in case of nuclear war. Thank God the secret service hadn't dragged him onto that plane instead of Air Force One. He and Sharon would never have gotten a good night's sleep in the super-spy command center. It would've been worse than trying to sleep in a hospital.

The President's cell phone buzzed again. Dutch kicked himself for getting talked into accepting an iPhone. His staff now controlled his attention 24/7. At least prior to the phone, they had to wait for him to wake up in the morning before giving him his marching orders. Now they could reach into his sleep and jerk him back to reality whenever they saw fit. So many people relied on him, Dutch was afraid to turn the damn thing off, even at night.

It didn't matter anyway. He had barely slept, feverish with concern over the nuclear attack and the civil disorder in California. His mind had been flipping bits of information until the wee hours of morning, hungry to connect the dots.

Dutch hunted around blindly in the dark stateroom, trying not to wake Sharon, until he found his reading glasses on the nightstand next to the bed.

"Jesus, God in Heaven," he swore, reading the first text on his phone.

"What's wrong, Dutch?" Sharon asked, startling awake.

"Homeland Security thinks we're being hit with a cyberattack. Power plants along the east coast are now having problems. When people start waking up in the east, we could be in for more power outages."

"Who?"

"Who's attacking us? We don't know, but the usual suspect would be Russia. They've probed our power systems before and they managed to shut down Ukraine's power grid a couple years ago."

"Why would they hit us?" she asked, sitting up in bed.

"The Russians are like that. If they sense weakness, they don't let the opportunity pass them by, even though tanking our economy would likely tank theirs." Dutch moved around the room, searching for clothes. Sharon turned on the reading light to make it easier for her husband to dress.

"Will we retaliate?"

Dutch chuffed. "Not unless we have proof, and I'm guessing we have bigger fish to fry today. Six metro areas in California rioted through the night. California State Guard is having trouble putting down the civil disorder. Apparently, only sixty percent of their guardsmen showed up for duty last night. They're not sure how many more will make it in today."

Dutch slipped on a clean undershirt and pulled on a track suit he found in a drawer. Like everything else in their life, someone had thought through this potential outcome ahead of time and stocked the presidential suite with clothes for he and Sharon.

He brushed his teeth and waded into the early morning maelstrom of the conference room, his gray and white streaked hair sticking up in the back.

"What's the situation?" Dutch took note of the staffers who had probably been awake most of the night, or at least since Homeland called in the cyberattack. His entire staff, plus the Attorney General, were present.

SecDef Greaney wasn't there, but Dutch doubted he had slept much either, not with a cyberattack underway. As suspected, Sam Greaney appeared in the doorway sipping a mug of coffee. He had probably been upstairs in the communications center.

"Good morning, Mister President," Robbie, his chief of staff, began the brief. "As you saw in my text, Homeland Security detected a virus working its way through our power companies and their transfer points starting at 3:35 a.m. Eastern Daylight

Time. Homeland is organizing a response, but the virus has been self-replicating, and we can assume that it's present in every power grid system across the nation and the eastern half of Canada."

"Have we launched our counter-measures?" Dutch had been briefed on a possible cyberattack on the power grid, and he knew that Homeland Security had prepared a defensive response.

"Well, this virus caught Homeland doing a scheduled update on their systems. They won't be back online until 8 a.m. Eastern. By then, the worm may have generated too many iterations in the system to isolate it."

Dutch glowered. "Why the HELL did DHS run a system update the night after a nuclear strike against the country?"

Robbie quailed at the unusual display of anger. "I'm sorry sir, but nobody in management told the programmers to hold off on the computer update. Those programmer guys kind of live in their own world. They will eventually eradicate the virus, but it won't be as quick as if we'd responded immediately. Homeland anticipates about fifteen days of power interruptions before they get it under control."

Dutch dropped into one of the chairs around the conference table.

"What else?"

"California is requesting federal troops. Last night, they reported rioting and looting in..." Robbie looked down at a list he'd written on a yellow legal pad, "Los Angeles, Santa Ana, Sacramento, Oakland, San Jose and San Diego. They're due to report in at 8 a.m. Pacific to assess damage and to discuss rules of engagement, but the governor forewarned us that they would be requesting federal troop support."

"Careful," Zach Jackson, Attorney General, interrupted. "Congress altered the Posse Comitatus Act during the Bush administration and then repealed it. We don't have the same free hand that they had back in the Los Angeles riots."

Dutch narrowed his eyes but said nothing.

"That isn't all, Mister President," his chief of staff turned to Sam Greaney, as though they had already discussed the next piece of information. "Other cities are experiencing sympathetic riots based on what social media is calling 'racially-biased distribution of electrical power.' They're convinced that the power companies are channeling available electricity to white, upscale neighborhoods, and they claim to have proof in the form of videos posted on Facebook, Instagram, Twitch and Twitter. We're getting reports of minor looting last night in nearly every major metropolitan city in the United States. Tonight, it might get worse."

"Let me make sure I'm getting this straight," Dutch bristled. "Cities without interruption to their electrical service are rioting because of some *racial bias bullshit* in other cities that they heard about on Facebook?" He leaned forward in his chair, fury now coming off him in waves.

"Yes, sir. The movement already has a name." Robbie looked down at his notes. "They're calling it 'Fair Power.'"

Dutch threw himself back in his chair. "People are probably dying from radiation poisoning from a *nuclear attack* on our country, and people in Chicago are rioting because they think some races are getting more electricity than others *in Los Angeles*? Is that what I'm hearing you say? Because this is *not* how America responds to an attack on our soil! We proved that with 9/11."

The president's staff shuffled their feet and looked anywhere but at their leader. Most of them were younger than Dutch by a fair margin. Two people in the room were Millennials. It seemed that the only person in the Oval Office who didn't understand how much America had changed since 9/11 was The President of the United States.

Sam Greaney sipped his coffee, still standing in the hallway, leaning against the bulkhead of the airplane.

Dutch calmed himself and turned toward his secretary of defense, the closest person to his age in the conference room. "Sam. What do we know about the nuke?"

"Well, Mister President, we know it was a baby nuke, probably something from when we were making devices that could fit into a piece of luggage. We have a location on all of ours, so that leaves a short list of possible provocateurs. It'll take some time to winnow down the list. We're spinning up ospreys this morning out of Twentynine Palms with Marine Corps radiation experts and flying them to ground zero in L.A.. We can't get anything into Los Angeles that wasn't already there by ground because half of Southern California is trying to drive out of the state, all at the same time. And the majority of cars will be running out of gas en route. It'll take weeks to clear the blocked roads."

"What do we know about the *people,* Sam? How many died because of the bomb? What's our radiation exposure?" Dutch fired back.

"Hardly anything, really. Our best guess right now is that we might have lost eighty people, mostly those in boats and others who crashed their cars because of the flash. The California civil authorities are barely picking up their phones in the Los Angeles area, presumably because the place is like Mogadishu right now. We'd love a chance to get some eyes on Los Angeles Harbor from the Coast Guard, but they're scrambling to put together a HAZMAT team from Monterey four hundred miles to the north. There used to be a Coastie HAZMAT team in Los Angeles Harbor, but less than half those guys are answering their phones, and the Coast Guard base got blown all to hell by the blast. The Coast Guard uses union dock workers to get their boats underway, and you can bet dollars-to-donuts that none of those union guys are going to show up right after a nuke. Cell service in L.A. is working fine, actually, but a lot of people aren't answering their phones right now. They're busy freaking out, I guess."

"So, we won't know the radiation exposure until your team from either Monterey or Twentynine Palms gets there?"

"Correct, Mister President. But the winds are favorable— SoCal is getting Santa Ana winds, which are hellacious for wildfires, but good for fallout. We're speculating that most of the particles from the nuke are blowing out to sea. The bad news is that the civil disorder in town has sparked fires that are now blowing into full-fledged wildfires."

"I know we already deployed FEMA to the site. When do they arrive?"

Silenced stretched until the president gave in. Apparently, nobody wanted to vouch for FEMA.

"Robbie, will you please find out where FEMA is? Americans might be dying from radiation exposure as we speak. I want to know how long it'll be before we turn this thing around."

"Yes, Mister President," Robbie vacillated between leaving the Oval Office or staying to take further orders.

"All bullshit aside, Mister President," Sam Greaney took another sip of his coffee. "FEMA's not going to get into L.A. anytime soon. Their air assets are skeletal, and they can't do anything without semitrucks. There's not a single road in or out of Los Angeles that isn't choked, balls-to-butt with abandoned vehicles, or will be by this afternoon."

The attorney general spoke up. "I'm concerned about the Marine Corps radiation team flying into L.A.. Will they be armed? Their presence might be construed as a violation of the Insurrection Act if they conduct an armed mission within the

U.S.. There's a small carve out in the law for using federal troops to secure fissionable materials, but I'll have to check on that..."

"Zach," the president talked over the top of his attorney general. "We're friends, right? So you know I mean it with respect when I tell you to shut the fuck up. I need you to be less of a lawyer and more of a patriot right now."

"I sure as hell hope you have solutions, Sam, because I'm sick of dead ends and colossal fuck ups," the President continued his tirade as soon as the door to the Oval Office closed behind his retreating staff. Sam Greaney, Secretary of Defense, braved the President's meltdown without any apparent bump in his blood pressure.

The plane did a small shudder, causing Sam to steady his coffee to keep from spilling it on the president's rug.

"I have solutions, Dutch, but you're not going to like them," the SecDef drawled.

"I'm up for absolutely anything that saves lives and gets us back on our game. Are you going to hit me up about counter-strikes against the Russians?"

"No, Mister President. That's the long game. We don't have the luxury of playing the long game right now. Nothing we do against the Russians is going to stop the virus that's already in our computers, and I doubt the Russians will mount an analog attack. They don't need to do anything more. We're doing a great job of screwing one another on Facebook and Insta-whatever."

"Then what's next on your list?"

"I've already given the Fifth Fleet a warning order that they'll sail for the states in five days and the Third Fleet is already steaming for home in Southern California. I'm frankly more worried about the inner-city riots. In my mind, they're the critical threat."

Dutch always had a sneaking suspicion that Sam Greaney was a bit of a racist, so he cocked his ear, preparing to take this next part with a grain of salt.

"I believe we might be facing a social media, psych warfare attack from our enemies. Probably Russia. Maybe China. Quite possibly both. This bit about 'Fair Power' reeks of a social media play by the Russians. They pit us against each other on issues of race or hashtag-*blah, blah, blah* and we never fail to take the bait. Most Americans strut around thinking it was our idea. The CIA knows for a fact that the Russians are manipulating us through social media, but we just don't know how much."

Dutch McAdams didn't think it was very much, but he let his SecDef keep talking. If he knew the man, the punchline was coming.

"We need to drop the hammer on these riots, before social media eats our lunch. Right now, we're getting just a little taste of the chaos that's on deck. Wait until those blackouts hit the big cities of the Midwest and the East. The race-baiters are going to lose their minds. Our troops need to roll NOW. When the droopy-pant gangbangers wake up from their night of looting and partying, they need to see Humvees with belt-fed machine guns outside their windows. Either we do that, or tonight's going to be hellfire."

Sam hadn't said anything that surprised Dutch. His SecDef had let his inner bigot fly, if only a little bit. Sam had been ideologically primed to blame the decline of America on racial minorities and inner-city criminals. For his part, Dutch sensed that American moral decay went a lot deeper than gangbanger criminals and welfare mamas, but a lot of what Sam said about race riots resonated with Dutch. He couldn't deny the threat of toxic ideas.

Even so, Dutch preferred to let this play without taking military action. Sam Greaney was right: something needed to be done immediately or the power failures from the cyber-attacks would cause social unrest to skyrocket. But it was Dutch's job to find a third way—a middle course that would stop short of ordering Americans to point guns at Americans.

"Okay, let's take a sanity break and meet here in fifteen minutes. Bring Zach in. I'm guessing there'll be some legal issues and he's going to insist on having a say."

6

I t never ceased to amaze Dutch how Sharon could compartmentalize stress. While he had been dealing with an existential threat to the United States, his wife, daughter and son had been looking through old photo albums back in the guest section of Air Force One. Sharon must have grabbed the albums when their secret service detail scooped them up for emergency transport to Andrews. Sharon always took the long view for the family. If the country was going to be nuked, she damn well wasn't going to lose the photo albums.

"Daddy, I didn't know you were a mountain man," Abby gleamed at her father.

"That's overstating things a bit, honey," Dutch rested his hand on the back of her auburn hair, taking emotional refuge in her youth and beauty. He and Sharon had gotten a late start on parenting; both getting through college, grad school and a good chunk of their careers before beginning their family. During the married-without-children time, Sharon earned her degree in clinical psychology, which had unexpectedly become a secret weapon during Dutch's career in politics.

"Your father spent several summers working as a hiking

guide for an outfitter out of Lone Pine, California, *the Gateway to the California High Sierras*. All summer long, he'd hike people up the highest peak in the continental United States, Mount Whitney," Sharon smiled at Dutch, no doubt remembering the summer they first met on one of those hikes. By the look in her eyes, he was ninety-nine percent sure they were both thinking about the same hammock, a bit off the same hiking trail, on the same cool, summer day in the Grouse Creek drainage. It was a minor miracle they were both virgins when they married two years later.

"Dang, Daddy, you were a babe!" Abby said, a little too loud. Several of the secret servicemen chuckled in the row behind the first family.

"My dad made me take that summer job. He thought I was growing up a little too privileged. He said that no son of his would be raised with a silver spoon in his mouth."

"Hey, that's the same thing you say to me," Teddy chided, softly punching the President of the United States in the shoulder.

"I say that because my dad was right. Who knows how I would've turned out if it weren't for that summer job. Sometimes, that's what it takes to become a man—the school of hard knocks teaches you some things you can't learn any other way." Dutch couldn't help but insert a bit of parenting agenda into the conversation. He'd been trying to talk his son into joining the Marine Corps for two years. Instead, Teddy meandered his way through his undergrad, studying French at Boston University.

"Well, there're many ways to get there," Sharon tempered. "Grandpa Chuck preferred the gritty, cowboy path, which is probably why they still live on a ranch."

"So you rebelled against the mountain life, Dad?" Teddy counter-argued. "You moved to the East, went to Princeton and became a Boston man? Everyone thinks you were born and bred in Massachusetts."

Dutch stepped back and rested his hand on Teddy's shoulder. "But I've got the gravel trails of the California High Sierras in my soul, buddy...enjoy the photos. Don't miss the one where I've got my shirt off. Your old man once had a six-pack." Dutch threw a quick jab that became a feather slap on the side of Teddy's head. "I love you guys."

Sam Greaney came marching down the hallway toward Dutch and his family, pushing shockwaves of urgency ahead of him.

"Dutch. The Saudis just buried the Iranians in a massive airstrike, probably reacting to the dirty nuke against their pumping station. The Iranians are mounting what retaliation they can. So far, nobody's hit Israel, but things are heading that direction."

Dutch put his hands on his hips and stared out the tiny window, searching for answers in the clouds. He took a deep breath and followed Sam Greaney toward the communications center.

7

"Dutch, you can't use federal troops in American cities. They are mostly protests. With the *possible* exception of L.A., you don't have legal justification." Zach Jackson stepped back from the president's desk with his hands on his hips. "President Bush and Congress modified the Insurrection Act to allow the president to call in federal troops to fight terrorism in the United States, but that ENTIRE amendment was repealed in 2008. *Gone*. Like it never existed. And there's no way to get Congress to pass something like that on the timeframe you need. The House and Senate are tossed to the four corners of the earth right now. Can't you use state guard to contain the protests?"

"We've already seen what happened in California with guardsmen," Sam Greaney argued, wiping his face with the handkerchief he kept tucked in his pocket. "They've been totally combat-ineffective. They can't even get their weekend warriors to report, much less execute on a coordinated mission."

"But not all states will be as uneven as California," Dutch pointed out.

"Sure," Greaney chimed in. "Some states have crackerjack

guard units and they might slam the door on rioters *in those states*, but what about the others? Social media shows up in every corner of the nation. *Those people*—the ones we're fighting here—have real time coordination. We need to take control of this situation and stamp it out everywhere, all at once. We can't abide half-assed solutions, and it's got to happen tonight. Federal troops are the only force with the command and control we need."

Silence descended as Dutch thought it through. A year from now, when the urgency and fear of this day was just a vague memory, he would be called upon to answer for this decision. He'd seen it happen after 9/11. The nation had galvanized and taken action after the tragedy, but the unity didn't last forever. Things returned to normal. People forgot. Congress returned to its aisles. At some point in the future, accountability would be measured out, especially when the Democrats had some time to think it through. If he broke the law now, it would end his career and taint his legacy.

"I need you to find me a way, Zach," Dutch weighed in. "I think it'd be unrealistic to trust the people, or even the states to clean up this mess on their own. The job falls to us. We're the ones who hold the levers of the greatest political and military force in the history of the world. We can *make* this turn our way. Unless we employ the right amount of force in the right places, things could spiral out of control. Let's get to work. I need legal justification to send troops into our cities and I need it now."

8

A s the day wore on aboard Air Force One, reports of the outages on the East Coast rolled in like a Biblical plague. Some technologically-savvy staffer set up an electronic map of the United States on the big screen in the conference room, and the power outages burned black holes in the otherwise chestnut map.

Orange County, Los Angeles and San Diego were dark. Initially, it had been the Delta, Utah power plant that had caused the outage, but now civil disorder in Southern California raged unchecked, and power failures were occurring due to violence, absenteeism and destruction of public works. The only good news was that blackouts weren't Southern California's biggest problem anymore. The mass exodus out of the region created a much bigger problem, and it wouldn't matter now if the power came back on or not.

The blackouts east of the Mississippi were bumbling around the map like a dog who'd stolen too many rum balls. Depending on the power engineering software used in any given part of the grid, and the state of maintenance of that software, the virus made more or less headway against security countermeasures.

Power companies employed a perplexing array of software solutions—DigSilent, SKM, ERACS, CYME, ETAP, RSCAD and PSSE, just to name a few. The virus penetrated software like a lothario working a singles bar. First, it would try a pick-up line, then buy drinks, next, hit on the "ugly friend." Eventually, the virus got into everyone's pants.

Cincinnati and the surrounding areas were almost entirely spared, thus far. Baltimore and D.C. had gone entirely dark. The Carolinas and Georgia were experiencing rolling brownouts. In Indianapolis, they couldn't even connect with cell phones—everything had gone down.

That made Dutch think about his in-laws. Sharon's parents lived in Indianapolis in a posh retirement community twenty minutes outside the big city. The president got up from his chair and walked back to his family.

"Sharon, have you had contact with your folks?"

She looked up from the paperback novel she was reading. His wife loved thrillers, this one with a shadowy figure with a pistol on the cover. "No, I didn't think we could call out on our phones during a WarFlight exercise. At least, that's what they told us in the briefing."

"I'm pretty sure you can connect in the comms center upstairs. They'll manage the security. Go call your folks. I'm worried."

"Is there a problem?" Sharon put down her book and unbuckled her seatbelt.

"The blackouts are hitting Indianapolis pretty hard. Let's see if their cell phones work. They're not getting connectivity within the city. Maybe Indianapolis didn't have as good a battery backup system. Or maybe the virus got into the cell networks."

Dutch and Sharon walked forward together toward the stairs at the front of the plane.

"What about your mom and dad in Bishop? Are you concerned with what's happening in California?"

Somebody had been keeping Sharon briefed, Dutch noted.

"The town of Bishop is a hell of a long ways off the beaten path. I'm sure they're getting some refugees up the backside of the Sierras, but I'd hate to be the guy who pushed his luck with my old man."

"Still...I'll go ahead and call them too." Dutch and Sharon arrived at the staircase and Sharon climbed toward the comms center while Dutch continued on to the Oval Office.

"I think I've found a way to justify troops," Zach Jackson announced. "But I can't guarantee it'll keep us out of trouble when Congress resumes. Protests are not the same as riots, and we've never seen a president respond to civil disorder with troops in EVERY major city. We could potentially be prosecuted."

Like all lawyers, Zach generally couched things in terms of absurd future risk. Never had a president been incarcerated for a crime.

"Go on..." Dutch nodded to his attorney general.

"We can take two approaches. The Obama administration passed this bit of language where we can claim that there is a threat of radiological weapons being used against major U.S. cities. We don't have any evidence of a threat other than the L.A. bomb, but that's a carve out from Posse Comitatus and we can use it. It's weak, but if we combine it with the stated purpose of the Insurrection Act—to prevent national rebellion—we could buy ourselves some wiggle room. It's not entirely without precedent. They used the same logic to send in Army and Marines during the D.C. riots in '68 and the L.A. riots in '92. We don't have widespread riots to back us up, but hopefully, by the time troops are in position, you'll have the riots you need."

"Jesus, Zach. I'm hoping to stop riots, not *use* them."

"Then I don't know what to tell you. If you stop the riots before they happen, then our legal justification evaporates."

"What about the looting last night?" Dutch challenged.

"That helps, but it wasn't enough to trigger states to call up guard units outside of California. It's a huge stretch to call them riots, especially when they're protesting racially-biased utility access. And I assume you'll be sending troops into other cities that have no rioting at all. To my knowledge, we don't have an invite from any governor or mayor other than California's." The attorney general held out his hands. "That's all I've got. There's non-inconsequential legal risk here, Dutch."

"Thank you, Zach. What are our next steps?"

"I need to draw up a request for Sam to send troops to intercept nuclear devices that we both know don't exist. Unfortunately, I'll have to sign the request myself, so it looks like you and I are in this together."

"Well," the President joked, "if we wind up in prison, I'll let you have the bottom bunk. How's that sound?"

"That doesn't sound funny, Mister President."

Sam Greaney knocked on the door and walked into the awkward pause in the conversation.

"What's the news? Are we rolling tanks or not?" Sam challenged, oblivious to the tension in the room.

Dutch tried to clear his mind, flipping back to a montage, three years earlier as he stumped along the campaign trail across the American South. He imagined the cities, waking up one by one as the sun rose across the country.

Charleston. Atlanta. Montgomery. Baton Rouge. Houston.

He pictured the young punks, sleeping off a night of mischief, in their beds, still living under their mothers' roofs in crowded low-income housing. He pictured the single moms, alone in their mass-built duplexes on the fringes of the cities, wondering when the electricity would return. He thought about African American children, frightened at the kitchen table, staring at a box of cereal, tuned to their parents' concern. He saw the retired pastor he'd met in New Orleans, his wife having just passed away. Dutch saw him wake up in his tiny urban home, flip the light switch and furrow his brow as nothing happened.

Dutch tried to take in all of America at once, three-hundred and twenty-five million people, and he weighed their fear, their vulnerability and their trust in him.

Most of them didn't understand the law or the Constitution. What they understood was food, water and electricity. They knew when their house was too hot or too cold. They knew when a flood, a fire or an invisible blanket of fallout threatened their children.

Those Americans could no longer care for themselves with the lights out, except in small pockets of hardy folk like his mom and dad. Most would expect the government to care for them, and right now, Dutch was the government.

They would want him to take command of the situation, regardless of the law.

"Sam. Send the Army into every city over 100,000 people. Send them armed, but I want a *total* weapons lockdown. This is a show of force, nothing more. Please do it now."

"Yes, sir." Sam Greaney set his coffee mug on Dutch's desk and walked out of the Oval Office.

10

A s Dutch contemplated the decision he had just made, alone in his office, a gentle knock on the door broke his reverie.

"Come in, Sharon."

"You okay, Dutch? You look shaken. And you need a shower." Sharon smiled.

It amazed Dutch how Sharon still took his breath away—the only person who would tell the President of the United States that he needed a shower. Sharon moved through the world like gentle storm, lightly refreshing the land, but capable of bringing focused destruction when necessary. Somehow, she had taken a moment to "freshen up" which meant she looked like a million bucks, despite being on an emergency WarFlight on Air Force One.

Even in her mid-sixties, Sharon kept her hair long and colored in the fashion of the day. Right now, she wore it slightly-platinum blonde with a darker shade at the roots. Dutch had no idea what to call the coloring, but he saw it on younger women in the political circles of power. Sharon had maintained an excellent figure, especially considering the natural drift of age.

She filled the role of first lady with impeccable poise and decorum, and everyone in the belt loop figured her for a beautiful political wife with a decorous, professional degree buried in her long-forgotten past.

Very few knew that Sharon was nobody to fuck with. Her indomitable will was a weapon she kept in her psychologist's tool box, rarely bringing it into the light of day.

"Hey babe. How are your parents?" Dutch stood and maneuvered her over to the couch so they could sit together.

"They're not answering their phones. The communications officer said that nobody in that region is connecting via anything other than satellite phone. They're beginning to think that the cyberattack included a hit on the older cellular networks."

Dutch took a deep breath and lifted Sharon's hand. "And my mom and dad. Are they good?"

"They're not answering either. I tried the home phone and both their cells."

"That's strange," Dutch worried aloud. "I can't imagine where else they'd be."

"Sam Greaney was up in comms when I made the calls. He offered to send troops to check on both our parents. Dutch, are you sending troops into the cities?"

"They're going in on weapons hold. We're launching a show of force to tamp down looting and rioting."

"Hmm," Sharon pursed her lips. "Weapons hold? Sounds like something Sam talked you into."

Dutch gritted his teeth. He rankled a little when Sharon second-guessed him like that, even if no one else was listening. It made him sound like a puppet, and he was nobody's puppet.

"It was my call and my call alone. Activists on social media are claiming that the power outages are a calculated act of oppression against the racial minorities. Rioting tonight could get out of control."

"And the people are believing it? That the blackouts are intentional?"

"Not quite. The activists are saying that available power is being channeled to white neighborhoods and away from low income areas."

"You should tell the nation it's a cyberattack."

"Good idea. Actually, it's a great idea. We've been hoping the power outages would be less severe and that we could write them off as too many air conditioners running at the same time. If Americans hear that we're under attack, they're likely to come together and stop burning their cities."

Sharon didn't look entirely convinced. "We'll see. I hope it was okay with you that I let Sam send troops to our parents' homes. I know how you hate special treatment."

That made Dutch think about the track suit and the extra clothes stored in the closets and drawers in the executive suite on Air Force One. He wondered what had happened to the clothing of previous presidents? Peril loomed over America and Dutch worried about wasted resources.

"We just need to get through tonight and everything should be okay."

Again, Sharon made that face, the one where her eyes glazed over in thought, her cheeks going a little slack.

"What?" Dutch asked.

"I'm just thinking about what you said concerning the social media rumors and electricity. That can't possibly be true, can it?"

Dutch harrumphed. "Not hardly. The only thing less likely than the power companies coordinating to screw the minorities would be the power companies coordinating to protect their own damn computer systems. Doing anything in this beast of a system takes about fifty times more effort and luck than anyone would imagine. I can't even get FEMA to move their asses into a nuclear strike zone in a timely manner, and I'm the damn president. There's no chance that the power companies are being cute. They have no motive, for one thing."

Sharon held out a hand to Dutch. "Right. But how is it that people have become so jaded and quick to assign malicious intent? Life's been pretty amazing for the past fifty years, hasn't it? Why do people turn to believing the worst in one another so quickly?"

Dutch held Sharon's thin hands like a lifeline. "Even thirty years ago, I think I could've predicted how Americans would react to a crisis like this. Something changed, and now I'm not so sure. So many times in our history, when the chips were down, Americans have come together and defeated evil. We're facing one of those times again, Sharon, and it came on *our* watch. And this time, when the Lord takes the measure of our virtue, I'm no longer sure where America will stand."

"What am I looking at?" Dutch asked Sam Greaney as he stared at the LCD screen in the conference room of Air Force One. Dutch and Sam sat at the polished mahogany conference table.

"I've had the tech geek overlay the map of troop deployments against our map of power outages. The troops are orange and the blackouts are black."

"Looks like Halloween," Dutch observed. "Why are the orange spots all just dots?"

"We're still in the process of issuing orders and mobilizing forces, sir. Most of the troops haven't left base yet."

"It doesn't look like any of them have left base. How long since they received orders?"

"Some of them, in the last hour." The secretary of defense looked at his watch.

"Some of them?" Dutch asked.

"Orders pass through channels sir, especially with something this unconventional," Sam explained.

"What aren't you telling me, Sam?"

"Some of the unit commanders are questioning the orders—

seeking confirmation that they're actually supposed to march on U.S. cities."

"We're not asking them to *shoot* civilians," Dutch emphasized, his hands clenching. "How many officers are questioning our orders?"

"It's hard to say. Most of them at first. But we need to give this a little time, Dutch. I'm sorting through those who will and those who won't take orders and making changes where they're needed."

"What does 'making changes' mean, Sam? Are you firing officers who object to our orders?" Dutch knew the answer already. The situation had grown hairier than anticipated, and it had only taken a couple hours.

Sam's face flushed red. Some men never did take well to following other men, Dutch reminded himself. Sam didn't answer Dutch's question, which was answer enough.

Dutch stood. "Sam, I want to be clear on this: if an officer objects to my orders on constitutional or legal grounds, he is NOT to be reprimanded or his career tarnished. Not in any way. Are we in agreement?"

"Mister President," the SecDef exhaled, gathering a head of steam. Sam Greaney began to raise his voice. "I need you to understand this, Dutch, in no uncertain terms: if we do not enforce your orders with swift action, we *cannot* expect to complete this mission. And I should remind you that the mission is to *save the United States!*"

"Do you think I don't know that, Sam? I'm trying to put this in the context of history—about what happens a year from now when everyone's forgotten how damn scary—"

"History?" Sam interrupted, shouting. "Wake up, Dutch! There won't be any fucking history if we don't *shut this rioting down right fucking now!*"

Dutch felt rather than heard thundering footsteps down the

hall. The doors burst open and his secret service detail swept the room with their Glock 17s. They didn't point their handguns at the secretary of defense, but they didn't point them entirely away from him either.

"Stand down, gentlemen," Dutch ordered, his hands held out in front of him. "Everything's fine here. We're just working through some hard choices. Please return to the security section." Dutch herded the four men toward the hallway. "Sam's just blowing off steam. Everything's fine," Dutch repeated.

As his secret servicemen backed into the hallway, they came up against the secretary of defense's security detail in military kit with AR-15 rifles dangling across their stacks of rifle magazines. Two of the four secret servicemen rotated to confront the Delta operators as though they were a threat to the president. The other two kept their guns pointed in the direction of the conference room. The Secret Service had formed a circle around Dutch.

"Whoa, whoa, whoa. I'm ordering *all* of you to go back to your seats. Immediately. Holster those weapons," Dutch shouted.

Sharon appeared, peering out from the executive suite. A handful of others from the presidential staff goosenecked into the hallway, alarmed by the ruckus.

More slowly than he would've preferred, Dutch's secret servicemen returned their handguns to their shoulder holsters, yet they remained in a protective posture. Dutch physically pushed them into the hallway, stepped back into the conference room and closed the doors behind him. On the other side of the door, he hoped everyone was ratcheting down their testosterone and returning to their seats.

"Control yourself and act like a goddamn professional," Dutch seethed at Greaney. "This is no time to lose your cool."

Dutch smoothed his tie. "Now, how do you propose to handle objectors? I want to know exactly what you're planning to do with those officers."

As evening descended on the Eastern seaboard, President of the United States, Nathaniel "Dutch" McAdams spoke to America. His staff had debated delaying the speech until 5 p.m. on the West Coast so that more of the country could tune in, but with the power outages and the severe stock market interruptions, nobody was likely to be at work on the West Coast anyway.

The stock markets hadn't been open for more than twenty minutes total that entire day; with huge sell-offs causing the protective algorithms to halt trading within minutes of opening.

A new wrinkle had arisen to curse the equity markets. Considering the massive damage to California real estate, few insurance companies were safe from the threat of bankruptcy, and their stock values plummeted based on that uncertainty. Even though homeowner's insurance almost never covered atomic war, it almost *always* covered damage from civil disorder, and that was enough to send the value of insurance shares into a tailspin.

On top of regular homeowner's insurance, thousands of bond issues and other forms of insurance covered corporations, buildings and public works. Something called "re-insurance" covered the insurance companies from too many claims, and of course, those re-insurance mega-corporations were running for cover now as well. With Southern California quite possibly devastated, the markets for bonds, securities and insurance were in free fall.

Runs on banks had become commonplace. Although it was Wednesday, comparisons to the Black Friday of the Great Depression rang across news channels, and the media settled on the catchy, but unhelpful moniker of *Black Autumn* to describe the sudden, terrifying fall of the financial industry.

Blackouts in the East rolled back and forth, not leaving the East and Midwest entirely without power, but depriving people of any confidence that the power grid would return. Dutch began to suspect that the Russian hack, if it was a Russian hack, was intentionally designed to keep them guessing.

In his speech, Dutch decided to bet all his chips on honesty with the American people. And if honesty failed, he would cash in on anger.

"My fellow Americans," the historic speech began.

Dutch told America the whole story insomuch as he knew it. He revealed everything he knew about the nuclear attack—that it had been a small bomb with few casualties and that the radiation readings showed no appreciable risk to Los Angelinos, particularly if offshore winds held. He told America about his suspicions that Iran had been responsible for the attack on Saudi Arabia. Then, Dutch told America about the cyberattack and his personal belief that a foreign nation had used a hack to capitalize on America's current misfortunes.

Dutch pled for calm. He begged people to return to their homes and their jobs. More than anything, he urged law and order.

Dutch addressed the question of "Fair Power" directly and

assured the American people that he had personally telephoned several CEOs of power companies, and he had received their assurances that everything possible was being done to provide electrical power to all people and in all neighborhoods.

Dutch laid it on the line, delivering one of the best, most authentic speeches of his career. By accounts among the staff on Air Force One, the speech bordered on heroic, and they broke into applause the moment after he signed off.

More than anything, Dutch told the whole truth.

Much later, as he looked back on the events of Black Autumn and on his speech, Dutch would conclude that everyone might have been better off if he had concocted a helpful lie instead.

"Mister President," Sam Greaney interrupted a late dinner between husband and wife.

"Yes, Sam?" Dutch wiped his mouth and steeled himself for news.

"At least seventeen major cities are in full-scale riot. I have troops in eleven of them and columns approaching two more. It didn't take long for the rioters to figure out that our men won't shoot, given that the rioters are well informed from social media. Our troops are unable to control the civil disorder. Mister President; we need approval to go weapons free, and we need it now or servicemen will die."

Dutch looked to Sharon, but other than her full attention, she had nothing to offer this dilemma.

"I'm going to need a minute to think about this, Sam." Dutch got up to move into his suite, his intention to pray.

"While you're both here," Sam hesitated, "I heard back from the teams we sent to your parents' homes. Sharon, your parents weren't there. Their condo complex appears to have been evacuated en masse and our team is trying to figure out where they went.

"Dutch, I don't know how else to say this, but we found your mother and father deceased in their home. I'm very sorry."

Dutch sputtered, "How can that be? They don't live anywhere near L.A.. They're hours from the city."

"The town of Bishop is only two hundred miles from Los Angeles—less than a tank of gas. My guys made it to your dad's ranch in a Blackhawk helicopter from China Lake in fifteen minutes. The roads were packed solid, and people from Los Angeles have been picking everything clean anywhere near a highway. It looks like your dad went down fighting. I had my men return your parents' bodies to the Naval weapons base nearby, awaiting your orders."

Dutch reached for the edge of the table to stop the world from spinning. His mom and dad were in their eighties, and Dutch had been preparing himself to lose them for a long time, and the fact that they had both lived into their eighties had been a blessing. Still, losing them both at once hit Dutch like a haymaker. "Could you please excuse us, Sam?"

"Of course." Sam closed the conference room doors behind him.

Dutch turned to Sharon, who had a hard look in her eyes, following Sam as he left the room. Seeing his grief, she softened. "Oh, Dutch, I'm so sorry."

"I can't believe they're gone. It doesn't make sense. I just spoke with my dad last week..."

"I'm sorry, Dutch." The couple held onto each other for a long time, letting the waves of grief wash over them. Sharon pulled back to look Dutch in the eyes.

"Dutch, I don't want to make this any harder than it is, but... your parents have a gate and a wall. They have loyal staff. Their neighbors are country people. Your dad refused secret service coverage because his ranch was already so secure. Are you buying this story?"

Dutch blinked away the fog floating around his head. "I hadn't thought about *not* buying Sam's story. There's no reason for him to lie... denial is a part of grief, Sharon."

"Maybe. But only two bodies? What about the others? Your mom and dad wouldn't have been fighting alone. A lot of people care about them and they wouldn't have left them alone with refugees marching down the highway."

Dutch didn't know what to say, so he said nothing. Sharon pulled her husband to the couch and sat with him while their dinner cooled on the conference room table.

_____

14

Dutch gazed at the E-4B Nightwatch through the bullet-proof glass window beside his desk in the Oval Office. It was just past 11 p.m., Eastern Time, and his staff had left him alone for an hour, no doubt giving him time to grieve his father and mother.

While Americans on the ground ran in fear from rioting, looting and fresh terrors, Dutch was left to grieve his 87-year-old father and mother. How many lives would this grieving cost? How many would die while the president got his personal shit together and headed back to business?

The Nightwatch plane blinked its mindless wingtip code of red and green. It looked like it was just off the wing of Air Force One, but Dutch knew that aeronautical distances were deceiving. The companion plane was probably more than a mile away.

Dutch understood Sharon's doubt of Sam Greaney. She had never liked the man—never fully supported Dutch's decision to tap him for SecDef. In her words, Sam Greaney always thought he was the smartest guy in the room. While Sam showed outward respect for Dutch's office as president, Sharon didn't buy it. She pegged him as a climber; a man pretending to defer to the Commander in Chief as a rung in his own ladder of ambitions.

Sharon had loved Dutch's mom and dad, maybe even more than Dutch loved them, and he had seen her do this before; letting emotions get out ahead of clear thinking. But Dutch could hardly blame her. The nation had plummeted into a downward spiral and all Dutch could do was dwell on his personal grief. Who was he to judge Sharon's emotional bias against Sam Greaney?

"Robbie, are you up?" Dutch hit the intercom on his desk and called back to the staff area.

"Yes, sir," Robbie answered, sounding like he hadn't slept in days.

"Please grab Janice and anyone else you need, and let's get to work. I'd like a brief on the rioting and the impact of the speech. Nothing fancy."

"Yes, sir. We'll join you in the Oval Office in five minutes."

Getting back to work satisfied his grief like four fingers of bourbon. He'd feel better for a little while, but there'd be hell to pay come three o'clock in the morning.

In five minutes, Robbie Leforth and Janice Foster sat in the Oval Office and Robbie began his brief.

"Mister President, I tried to gather response data from your speech tonight—I thought it was an amazing speech by the way, truly one of the great speeches of all time—but the polling firms have gone offline, and half the people called in sick from our NSA signals and intelligence group, which might not have mattered since they don't do consumer polling anyway. Usually, the media polls our moves, but they're either understaffed or focusing on their own ideological positions. I couldn't find any media polls relating to your speech. Basically, all I can show you is my own review of the social media reaction, which might be the most accurate, since we don't know how many people even had the ability to tune in on television. While cell batteries hold, and while cell towers continue to function, almost all media is being consumed on smart phones."

Dutch nodded for him to continue.

"On your personal Facebook page and the White House page, you got over one-point-seven million reactions, mostly 'likes.' There were over a hundred thousand comments and they expressed a lot of support overall. I did notice a substantial number of comments expressing distrust of your relationship with the electrical company CEOs, since you said that you called them personally. A substantial minority of comments criticized your motives as a 'white, patriarchal male' and made unflattering comments about you having the kind of friendship with large corporations where you could call them. But I emphasize that critical comments were in the *minority*."

"And what about the reality on the ground? What impact did the speech have on civil disorder?"

"We have reports of major rioting in seventeen cities, and we expect more before the evening is through. The riots in California have intensified. I don't think we can say Los Angeles is 'rioting' anymore because I don't think there's a coherent police presence in most of the Greater Los Angeles area. It's more like anarchy—"

A knock interrupted Robbie's report and Sam Greaney stepped into the Oval Office, his face set hard like the prow of a Greek fighting ship. "Dutch, we have lost our first military personnel. Three men were just killed in hand-to-hand fighting against rioters in Detroit." He handed Dutch a piece of paper that looked like a report of some kind. "It's now or never, sir," Sam prodded.

Dutch didn't like being backed into a corner, but he'd learned that sometimes you played the cards you were dealt. He might never know the ultimate impact of his speech, but it seemed clear at this point that the kind of people who rioted probably weren't the kind of people who watched speeches from the White House.

"Order our men weapons free," Dutch said, putting the nation and his presidency in God's hands.

15

"How much longer should we stay in the air, Sam?" Dutch ran into Sam Greaney walking down the hallway at first light.

"We just mid-air refueled and we're waiting for confirmation that the riots are under control. Going weapons hot stopped the bastards in their tracks, Dutch. Looks like we might have this licked."

"How many dead?" The President listened intently.

"I'm not sure. Sounds like two or three hundred dead in thirty cities, sir. We've suffered thirteen casualties among our military personnel, but I'm still waiting for reports. We are experiencing some...communications difficulties."

Dutch sensed something lurking beneath the words. "Tell me what that means, Sam."

"You already know that we lost a few officers over legal objections when we ordered them into American cities. I already covered most of those losses with inline promotions."

Dutch pictured the kind of men who would object to his order to shoot at civilians and couldn't help feeling like he might have been among them.

"A couple more commanders withdrew troops to their base when we made the call to go weapons hot. I'm working on getting those officers replaced. A couple of our bases have gone radio silent."

"Radio silent?" Dutch couldn't believe that the hardened military communications systems had been impacted by a cyberattack.

"Some of our bases and also units in the field have stopped communicating with us. Mister President, I'm guessing that some of them are objecting to orders and others are losing cohesion of force."

"What does that mean?"

"Sir, I believe we are experiencing absenteeism and desertion in some of our units, mostly admin and support. Combat troops are holding up better."

Dutch imagined how servicemen and women might feel about the power outages, the nuclear attack, the riots and the stock market crash. Many would have a strong desire to rally around their families rather than stay at their jobs. The ragged truth: their duty to family might be stronger than their oath to the country. Dutch could understand that feeling, especially today, with his father's body lying on concrete in an airplane hangar somewhere in the California desert. At some point, family would become everything, regardless of oaths.

"Why are we still in the air? We're seeing no missile launches, no ground forces and no planes threatening our airspace. Why aren't I on the ground talking to these officers personally?"

Sam paused and scratched his stubble. "Sir, we're seeing a statistically-manageable attrition rate in our forces. It's not like we need a hundred percent force to put down civilian riots. It's not as though they're armed with RPGs. You're missing the point: we're getting these cities under control. Please come look at the battle screen and you'll see what I mean."

They moved from the hallway to the conference room. The big screen TV looked like Christmas and Halloween had been thrown in a blender, then tossed on a map of the United States.

"I know the black areas are blackouts and the orange areas are troop concentrations. What are the red and green areas?" Dutch asked.

"Red areas are active civil disorder and green areas are pacified." Sam pointed to Detroit, which was still red with an orange blob at the periphery. Then he pointed to Atlanta, which was black with a green blob in the center. "We've pacified Atlanta, but we haven't pacified Detroit yet. There's a combined force of Michigan state guard and regular army from Fort Custer closing in on Detroit now. The jammed roads are slowing them down, but we expect they'll reach the city soon."

"Well, I can see why we're still in the air," Dutch tapped the screen over the Washington D.C. area, a large, red blot without any orange or green inside.

"The cyberattack seems to be hitting the area around D.C. particularly hard—Richmond has been dark for thirty-six hours and our forces at Fort Lee are entirely occupied with city-wide civil disorder there. To the north of D.C., Baltimore is an absolute shit-show. Andrews and the White House are hemmed in by four hot spots and the roads are blocked. The Marine Corps barracks at 8th and I St. have barricaded themselves in and they're waiting for mechanized support. Sir, we cannot land back in D.C. until we make some substantial progress in that area."

"Please walk me through the situation on the ground in D.C.. I need to understand what's happening."

"I'm not sure D.C. is a good example, Dutch. We've had an asymmetrical reaction to our peacekeeping force in some cities, including D.C.. Marines from Quantico immediately responded to my call to move on the White House, but they were on weapons hold, so they couldn't do much more than look nasty. Here's where it gets weird; they were driven back to their beachhead by a coordinated force of armed civilians—gangbangers, they thought. The Marines took a lot of incoming fire."

"What do you mean by 'a coordinated force of civilians?'" Dutch tried to picture it—gangbangers squaring off against Marines—and he couldn't.

"The Marine ground commander said that civilians were maneuvering on the Marines in a coordinated fashion, flanking their forces and trying to cut off their avenue of retreat. His exact words were that the civilians—'urban irregulars,' he called them—fought like Chechen Muslims in Iraq."

"Wait. He said they were Chechens—Russians?" Dutch interrupted.

"No. He thinks they were gangbangers. He later compared them to trained fighters. Chechens in Iraq were trained by the Russian military before becoming Islamic terrorists. In other words, the Marine ground commander thought that these gangster guys maneuvered like trained warfighters."

"Were enemy troops inserted into D.C.?" Dutch's worldview threatened to take a precarious turn.

Sam shook his head. "I don't think so. We're working a few theories. In any case, the Marines will crush them now that they're weapons hot."

"Tell me about the theories?"

"Nothing substantial. The CIA had a few uncorroborated reports of military age males from the gang population engaging in militia-like training in the woods of Virginia. We wrote it off as urban legend. Maybe we were wrong. Maybe some Mexican cartel was preparing to take advantage of civil disorder. The only entities we could think of who might do that would be the cartels or the Russians or maybe both."

"That's insane, Sam. Now you're sounding like one of those alt-right talk show hosts. I know you have a bit of a burr under your saddle about the blacks and Hispanics, but you don't actually believe this, do you?"

Sam Greaney shrugged. "Is anything really beyond the realm of possibility right now? Strange came out of the woodworks last night. Some smart criminal or maybe a rogue nation prepared for this. It's just a few hot spots in a few cities, but some of the gangbangers are more than just pissed-off criminals. They're insurgents. And social media isn't doing us any favors. They're recruiting much faster than we are."

"Until we're talking about more than just a couple of firefights, let's put these theories on ice, Sam."

Dutch didn't like his SecDef's worldview. The president had entered the zone of regret when it came to sharing leadership with Sam Greaney. Dutch reluctantly admitted to himself that he may have taken the "Team of Rivals" thing too far. He'd imitated the personal leadership style of Abraham Lincoln by building a cabinet of bullheaded critics and devil's advocates. It had played well for Dutch, but that didn't mean the strategy was bulletproof. His misgivings about Sam Greaney churned in his gut like last night's Thai food.

The racism thing was coloring Sam's judgment, but that didn't necessarily mean Sam was wrong. It did mean he was *insecure* though, and insecure people with power could be dangerous.

The conundrum wasn't worth pursuing. They had bigger problems than Sam's daddy issues—or whatever they were.

"There are a lot more troops around D.C. than just the Marines from Quantico. What're we doing to take our capitol back?"

Sam stepped up to the map, as though to show troop movements, but the scale was too large. Still, Sam pointed at Washington D.C., a red blob that bled into the red blobs of Baltimore and Richmond.

"There aren't as many combat troops as you might think near D.C., sir. We're tapping some ceremonial and administrative units, but they're still soldiers and Marines. First Battalion, Third Infantry is moving out of Fort Meyer to form a cordon to the south of the capitol and expand the zone of control southward toward Richmond. Mechanized and MP units out of Fort Bragg are en route, but they are experiencing delays due to massive traffic jams. When they get to D.C., they will set up a blocking force to the north, facing Baltimore. 91st Engineer Battalion from Belvoir will split in two and help the battalions from Meyer and Meade clear roads north and south, enforcing a growing area of order. They need to clear Highway 1 into D.C. first. That'll take a day, maybe two. Our ground units at Andrews are going to expand out from the base, linking up with the Marines and the D.C. Guard to create a protected corridor back to the capitol. The Marines at Quantico will serve as shock troops for the D.C. Guard in taking back the streets of D.C.. We've called up the Virginia Guard and they'll be joining with the Strykers at Fort Pickett to clear the 95 toward Bragg. We would like to get the 7th Transport Group from Fort Eustis in the game, but we're having trouble reaching their commander. Either he's tied up with civil disorder in Richmond or they're intentionally not returning our calls. Take your pick."

"When can we land?" Dutch asked again.

"I'm not sure that's a good idea, sir. There is no major command-and-control base with a big enough airstrip where I can guarantee your safety. If you land, it might generate a surge of protest among civilians. Men could die defending you. Virtually all major airbases are near population centers. I need more time to pick the right base and to create a buffer zone around it."

Dutch wanted to be part of the solution, not part of the problem. Landing at a new base might exacerbate the problem. Maybe he was more useful in the air, as miserable as it was.

"I'd like to land as soon as we have a reasonably secure landing area—somewhere I can take command and de-escalate the situation from the ground. In the meantime, what're we doing to get the stock market under control?"

"That'd be a question for Secretary Avenall. The last contact we had with him was ten hours ago in D.C.."

Dutch looked at D.C. on the television screen, a red area with tentacles reaching toward Richmond, Baltimore and even Frederick, Maryland, with the Secretary of the Treasury buried somewhere in the middle.

"Let's reach out to the Deputy Secretary of the Treasury, then. Thank you, Sam."

"No problem, sir. We'll win this. Things are looking good. Troops are on the move and they're making a difference." Sam Greaney again promised. "We have over four hundred thousand combat troops in-country, and no sane civilian throws rocks at a Stryker armored fighting vehicle."

16

L ike a nervous suitor at a father's door, Air Force One circled over the heartland of the United States, unable to return to D.C. and unwilling to give up its mission. Seven days after the crash of the stock market, the President and his retinue still hadn't touched ground.

Dutch had received three military briefings each day for the last seven days, and he had come to know the feeling of Thor, unable to lift his hammer.

Launching troops from their bases had triggered an entirely-unexpected effect: civilian truck drivers drove home and stayed there.

Such a devilishly-forgettable factor—uncomplicated men with a demanding job and significant autonomy. Truck drivers had no reason to risk themselves or their trucks in the midst of riots, during a military show of force.

The Los Angeles riots of 1992 had demonstrated the foolishness of a truck driver entering a city while it rioted. Reginald Denny had been dragged from of his semi-truck cab and beaten while news cameras filmed overhead, which forever burned one simple truth into the minds of truck drivers: there are no medals pinned to the chest for delivering product during a riot. Only potential beatings.

While Sam Greaney battled the current war—civil disorder from rolling blackouts—the next war slipped in under their noses. Within days, they faced catastrophic food shortages. Rioters were no longer hapless teenagers and opportunistic gangbangers. Now their mothers and grandmothers lined up to shout at the army and national guard troops. Rioting had gone mainstream.

What had once been demonstrations in a hundred metropolises became serious civil unrest in nearly every city over ten thousand people. A hundred riots became twenty-six hundred riots within forty-eight hours of sending troops into the big cities. Regular Americans could abide a power outage during early fall. What they could not abide was hunger.

The sheer size of the United States contributed to Dutch's defeat. 400,000 combat troops sounded like a massive number —enough to defeat any army in the world. But helicopter gunships and Tomahawk cruise missiles don't stop angry fathers and mothers, and troops on the ground can't be everywhere at once. In squads of thirty, 400,000 troops can only hold 13,000 street corners in 2,600 cities. If each city has a hundred such street corners, then infantry can only cover five percent of a city while desperate urbanites loot out the other ninety-five percent. Panic-stricken Americans didn't need to defeat soldiers in order to steal supplies. They only needed to move over to the next block.

Before the collapse, when doomsayers talked about grocery stores only having food for three days, they hadn't factored in hoarding. The moment blackouts extended past a couple of hours, people raced to the markets and vaporized everything remotely edible. Stores that attempted to lock their doors were broken down and overrun. People who came late for the frenzy went crazy with fear, committing criminal acts of petty violence and theft that would've been inconceivable a week earlier. The specter of empty shelves drove good people into a very bad place. And the panic devolved with each passing day, going from bad to apocalyptic.

Sam Greaney wasn't coming entirely clean about the state of the troops. Dutch had set up a back-channel communication with three Army generals—friends from college. In a half-dozen satellite phone conversations, Dutch gathered the truth: that absenteeism in the troops had skyrocketed. The "four hundred thousand American combat troops" had declined to something approximating half that number. Especially among national guard units, men and women returned to their families rather than guard street corners while they watched their own cities burn.

Robbie Leforth, the President's chief of staff, sat in the Oval Office on Air Force One and Dutch could smell him. Robbie looked like shit. While the President and first lady had a suite full of clothing, Robbie hadn't had a chance to grab more than the one suit he was wearing.

"What's the shower situation, Robbie?"

"I'm sorry, sir, but we're on severe rationing, and the flight crew is allowing only one shower per four days. I know I must look and smell awful."

Robbie had been an exceedingly loyal chief of staff, and somehow seeing his friend wrinkled and oily brought the nation's predicament all the way home for Dutch. Millions were suffering hunger and violence miles below the gleaming airship. The thought hung on Dutch like a clouded nightmare, a memory of some almost-forgotten sin. But his dirty assistant could not be denied, and he nearly brought tears to Dutch's eyes.

"You know, Robbie, you're a good man. I don't think I've ever thanked you for your service to this country," Dutch choked up.

"Thank you, sir. It's an honor, particularly to serve you."

Dutch waved away the compliment. "What's the latest news on your family?"

"Thank you for asking. Michelle and Regina are with my parents in Maine. I haven't heard from them in two days. The cell towers must've stopped working in that part of the state. As you know, Jeremy is stationed in Germany. I got through to him and he said something about Muslim immigrants causing trouble in Stuttgart."

Dutch furrowed his brows. Unchecked European immigration had been a ticking time bomb, and he could easily see Muslims rising from the civil disorder as an organized threat. Hopefully, he was wrong.

BOOM, SNAP!

Dutch heard a massive bang, something he had never heard before on an aircraft. He rushed into the hall and headed aft, where he could now hear screams and shouting. As Dutch rounded the corner of the conference room, he ran into two secret service agents who immediately threw him against the bulkhead and placed their backs to his, pinning him to the wall.

The shouting receded, and the screams turned to sobs. Dutch squirmed underneath the weight of the secret servicemen and worked his way out between them enough to capture the scene in the office staff section of the plane. Once again, the secret servicemen and the protective detail for the secretary of defense were pointing guns at one another. A man in a business suit lay face-down on the cabin floor, a huge burgundy pool beneath his head. Dutch's daughter, Abigail, stood hiding in Sharon's arms, weeping uncontrollably.

"Abby, are you okay," Dutch shouted over the din.

"Yes, Daddy. I'm fine. I'll be okay," she sobbed, then pitched into a fit of coughing.

"What happened?" Dutch demanded of the secret

serviceman still pinning him to the wall—Daniel Brooks, he recalled, the chief of his detail.

"Sir, the man on the ground grabbed your daughter and threatened her with a knife from the galley unless we landed the plane in D.C.. We refrained from shooting so as not to risk the integrity of the airframe, as we're trained, sir. This... cowboy, sir, took a shot with his M4." The secret service man pointed his chin at a Delta operator from the SecDef's detail.

"Okay. Relax, everyone." Dutch pushed his way from behind the agents and addressed the operator who had killed his daughter's assailant. "What's your story?"

"No story, sir. I had the guaranteed shot from behind the man and I took it. I'm shooting frangible ammo, so there was zero chance my round would compromise the aircraft after passing through his skull."

"What is frangible ammo?" Dutch demanded.

"Powdered metal compressed into a slug. It breaks up when it hits a hard target. There was little risk of over-penetration, and I had the shot, point-blank."

Dutch looked opposite where the man had apparently fired and could see a number of gray impact marks on the fuselage and bulkhead, along with a constellation of pink spackle. Dutch turned to his wife and daughter and shepherded them back toward their suite at the front of the plane, wrapping his arms around them as they walked. His son, Teddy, followed.

As he herded his family away from the specter of death, he remembered the words of his father when Dutch called him, late at night on the West Coast, to tell him he'd won the election to the presidency of the United States. His father's words had knocked Dutch off kilter and had haunted him as he worked long hours as leader of the free world.

"Congratulations, son. Just don't forget: you'll be president for four years. But, you will be a father and a husband forever."

Dutch ground his teeth as the words echoed in his soul, his daughter weeping hysterically, and Sharon wrapped around her like a shawl.

The ghost of his dad, apparently, had found him 30,000 feet above America.

17

Robbie Leforth, Zach Jackson, Sharon McAdams and the president sat in the Oval Office. Sam Greaney hadn't been invited. Late afternoon light cut through the windows, projecting fake rainbows on the plastic walls of the seat of power of the United States of America—or what was left of it.

"I have one question, and I need it to stay in this office. Why were Sam's men armed with frangible ammunition? I can only think of one reason, and it isn't good. I'm hoping the three of you can think of alternative explanations."

Dutch's attorney general seemed to connect the dots before anyone else in the room. "You don't think Sam had something to do with the attack on the United States, do you Dutch? I mean, he's an asshole, but a traitor? I can't believe that."

"I don't get it," Sharon said. "Why does having frangible bullets mean that Sam Greaney was in league with the cyberattack?"

"Maybe it doesn't," Robbie replied. "Maybe he just came onboard ready for violence."

"Back up." Sharon held out her hands in a stopping motion. "What am I missing?"

Dutch explained. "There's only one good reason to come loaded with ammunition that shatters on impact, and that's to be ready to shoot on the airplane. Not even the secret service was loaded for a shooting incident inside the fuselage."

Sharon slumped back on the sofa, thinking.

"Who was that guy? The one who grabbed my daughter?" Dutch asked as the silence stretched out.

"His name was Paul. He was one of my legal staff," Zach Jackson, the attorney general exhaled. "He hadn't heard from his family in D.C. in four days, and his stock portfolio had been completely wiped out by the first wave of sell-offs. He also didn't have a chance to bring his anti-depressants on board. I made him come with me even though he objected. I think all this is my fault."

Dutch shook his head. "When it comes to mental instability, it's hard to assign blame. How's everybody else on the plane doing? Paul probably wasn't the only one in a bad way."

Nobody answered, probably because everyone was feeling the stress, including each of the four in the Oval Office. Being cooped up in a beautiful, custom-built flying hotel could still feel like a prison, and everyone aboard had come to know that unexpected truth.

"We need to get on the ground and empty this airplane," Sharon stated. "Things are going to go from bad to worse in terms of mental health. Plus, if Sam Greaney is actually a threat, then we need to tie a rope around that threat."

18

As Air Force One descended toward Omaha, Nebraska, Dutch broke the news to Sam Greaney. As much as he would've liked to leave the man in Omaha, he would have to justify it based on a frayed suspicion triggered by the kind of ammunition his men had brought onboard. As Dutch well knew, there could be a hundred plausible explanations.

"You're going to need to ditch your security guys at Strategic Air Command, Sam. We're getting rid of everyone on the plane except for critical personnel. If we're going to have any chance of taking this country back, we can't be toting around a plane full of non-essential personnel distracting us from our mission. I've seen secret service guys point guns at your guys, and your guys point guns at them *twice* now. That's over. Your heavy hitters are Nebraskans now."

Sam Greaney's eyes narrowed as he seemed to consider arguing the point. Then his face relaxed. "Okay, Mister President, I will need four of my support guys, and of course the comms operators if we're going to continue coordinating the military effort."

"Okay," Dutch agreed. "Another thing, Sam. I'm going to need two hours on the ground to do my job as a father."

"How's that, Dutch?"

"If we can't get D.C. back in our control, and if we end up making a contingency landing somewhere else, I need to know I can take care of my family. As it stands, on this airplane, I don't even own a pair of jeans."

Sam raised an eyebrow. "You want to gather supplies for your family?"

"You can't guarantee the success of this mission and neither can I. At the end of the day, I'm a father. What kind of father would I be if I didn't prepare for my family's long-term options?"

Dutch could see the wheels turning in Sam's head. A little younger than Dutch, Sam's wife had passed away from breast cancer ten years prior, and his son worked as a business executive in London. Sam would struggle to see things from Dutch's perspective when it came to family. Sam seemed to reach some kind of decision and it made Dutch's shoulder's tense.

"Okay, Dutch. I'll have a quartermaster standing by ready to set you up with whatever you need at SAC base. They should be able to send you off with a damn Army/Navy Surplus store. That's where the 'doomsday preppers' buy their stuff, right? Army/Navy Surplus?" Sam laughed, and Dutch couldn't tell if he was being ridiculed.

"Two hours, Sam. I need to be a father for *two* hours. After that, I'm back to being President of the United States, and we can pull our country back from the brink. Deal?" Dutch disliked the sound of himself negotiating with his secretary of defense. He knew himself well enough to know that his self-doubt was eating away at his personal strength. Undoubtedly, his father and mother's passing had eroded that foundation. In the end, no man could be utterly certain of his mental fortitude. Depression could get its hooks into anyone.

"Of course, Dutch. It's no problem. You're President of the United States. You can take as many MREs as you want, whenever you want."

The intercom announced the return to seats as Air Force One lined up for landing.

Sam Greaney stood and moved toward the door. "Dutch, you might want to let Robbie Leforth off at Omaha as well. He's wearing a little thin."

19

As he sped across the tarmac in a Humvee, Dutch's mind tore at the problem like a dog scratching out a hole. What could he do in the next two hours that would ensure his family's long-term survival?

He had already decided that he should approach the problem as though America would never come back. It was the last thing he wanted to believe, but he owed it to his family to face that reality. For starters, he would have to frankly consider the end of the American nation and all the comforts that had come with it.

Not only would he have to imagine his world without modern advantages, but he would have to see it without him as president. In a desolate future, Dutch's role as leader of the free world would be a curiosity at best, a death warrant at worst. For seven days, hanging over America in the sky, Dutch had born witness to tens of thousands of fires, particularly as they passed over populated areas. From horizon to horizon, the hopelessness of Americans billowed into the air like blackened fists, thrusting their impotent wrath skyward only to dissipate in the coming jet stream of winter.

A hundred thousand pilasters of smoke offered final judgment on modern American city culture: they were not of a heart to redouble their efforts, tighten their belts and proceed forward with greater humility. This was not the America of the Great Depression, where most turned to growing vegetables instead of lawns, packing families into smaller homes for warmth, and scavenging trash for reuse.

In contrast, modern Americans set fire to their cities.

If he were recognized as president, their indignation and blame would likely sweep his family up like rats. It made him think of black and white photographs of Mussolini, the Italian dictator, hanging upside down with his mistress from iron scaffolding.

The thought made him glance at his driver, an Air Force supply management officer. The man stared straight ahead as he drove, wrapped in professionalism. Dutch couldn't tell if the man blamed his president for the sudden loss of his hopes and dreams.

The air whipping through the Humvee blew heavy with the smell of smoke, a grim reminder of the panic and disorder that had swallowed nearby Omaha. Dutch wondered how the man must feel about helping them take resources from their base. Those same resources could've otherwise contributed to the survival of the man, his base and maybe his family. Dutch felt an urge to ask about the man's family, and almost spoke. Instead, he clamped his mouth shut.

For these next two hours, he needed to put aside his concern for anyone other than his family and friends. For the next two hours, he would be a father again; maybe too late, but better late than never.

As the Humvee sped closer to the chain-link fence surrounding the airfield, Dutch reined in his thoughts. For the first time ever, he needed to focus on the animal survival of those he loved. He tapped that version of himself—almost fifty years in the past—that had lived in the hardscrabble world; a lifetime distant from when he worried about whether blue socks clashed with his charcoal slacks.

Dutch would have to locate that place in his soul that once scaled Mount Whitney, the lives of his hikers utterly reliant upon his judgment. In a past life, he once concerned himself with pack weight, calories, exertion, and above all else, weather. He would take in the capabilities of those in his care and assess their strength and needs, their boots and cardiovascular fitness. He would set contingency plans to ensure survival when Murphy's Law came to call and stacked against them all the worst-case scenarios and maybe some scenario he had never considered.

Dutch forced his mind to consider merciless nature and entropy; a heartless adversary who would fight his every move with random, dangerous permutations. All his education, experience and intelligence could come down to this moment and this question: what would he pack aboard Air Force One to save his family's lives?

Dutch had already decided they would not remain at Offutt Air Force Base. Earlier, as they'd descended from above the clouds in Air Force One, he'd seen the burning of Omaha—hundreds of fires, curling black-on-black tendrils into the sky. Something in Dutch's subconscious had known that those chemical fires bespoke a greater evil; that a malevolent legion would eventually come for his family if they stayed long at Offutt.

After doing all he could for his family to survive, Dutch might have to shrug off the mantle of president and go forward as any other man, fighting to protect his own.

Food was the first thing to come to mind, but Dutch held

that thought at bay for a moment, considering the minarets of smoke over Omaha.

"Guns." Dutch shouted to the driver over the howling wind in the Humvee. "Please take me to the armory."

The officer nodded with a slight smile, apparently approving of Dutch's awakening.

Security first. Everything else second.

20

Dutch, his son Teddy, the supply officer, and two Air Force security officers stood together for a moment, regarding the racks filled with modern firearms. Given the critical nature of Strategic Air Command to the defense of the United States, someone had seen fit to arm the base security forces to the teeth. Unfortunately, the array of weapons did more to confuse Dutch than inspire him.

"I'm really, *really* wishing you had taken my advice and joined the *damn Marines*, Teddy," Dutch said, half-jokingly. The three servicemen chuckled.

"Sorry, Dad. I'm pretty useless in this department," Teddy apologized. "Everything I know about this stuff I learned from Call of Duty."

Dutch had shot guns a lot growing up on the slopes of the California High Sierras, but his father's arsenal titled decidedly toward cowboy-style firearms. The scores of oiled, black rifles arrayed before him looked like movie props to Dutch.

"If I may, sir..." one of the Air Force security men spoke. Both he and the other security force officer were outfitted like Navy

SEAL assaulters: camouflage fatigues, kevlar helmets and chest rigs with magazines, radios and other doo-dads sticking out in all directions.

"Please do. I would consider it a favor," Dutch said, motioning to the racks of weapons.

The three airmen snapped to work loading up a rolling handcart for the president. They began with six, compact assault rifles, each with a chunky holographic sight on top. The men buzzed around the armory grabbing guns, ammunition, batteries, extra batteries; chatting it up like schoolgirls on a shopping spree at the mall. For a moment, Dutch forgot how deadly-serious this exercise might be. Even with America burning, it was hard to imagine he would ever defend his life and family with military hardware.

"Sir, how do you feel about this one?" One of the airmen held up a big, bolt action rifle with a hulking scope on top.

"If that's a Remington 700, then I think we're good to go," Dutch couldn't help but show off a little. When he was a young man, he had hunted deer in central California with a wood stock version of the same rifle.

"Excellent." The airman beamed approval and loaded the rifle in the cart. "This one's a 7.62, sir. I'll grab a case of ammo for it," he said as he darted into another room.

Finally, the supply officer brought out three crates full of hand grenades.

Dutch held up his hands. "I'm not sure grenades would make sense for us."

His son shook his head, smiling in a parody of disappointment with his old dad. "If I've learned one thing from hundreds of hours playing Call of Duty, it's that you never pass up on grenades." Teddy carefully took the crates from the waiting airman and loaded them into the rolling cart.

"I suppose that means Javelin and LAW rockets won't be required," one of the airmen asked.

"No, thank you," Dutch confirmed. "But I do think that night vision goggles and maybe some body armor could be helpful."

"Absolutely, sir. That stuff's next door."

21

Word spread that Air Force One had landed in Offutt, and Dutch's worst fears began to coalesce around the front gate to the base. The two security forces officers helping Dutch were pulled away to address a menacing crowd of angry civilians at the base entrance, shouting pleas and curses for their president to save them from the turmoil that had seized Omaha.

Dutch had no time to agonize over their ire. He had only an hour left on the ground and he wracked his brain as to what his family might need in the months to come.

Try as he might, he could not come up with a large-scale, reliable solution to providing clean water for his family. Every good option seemed tied to a piece of land. He needed a river, lake or a well to provide water for any length of time, and he had a bad feeling about setting up near ground water. It seemed like ground water would attract people, and that he must stay clear of the masses at all costs.

The more he thought about long-term survival, the bigger the problem loomed. Dutch felt like Alice falling down the rabbit hole—the questions becoming deeper and stranger the farther he descended. The president kicked himself for not preparing ahead of time, like setting up a ranch in Montana or a farm in a small town. He'd *had* the money. He just hadn't thought to make it a priority.

Ultimately, Dutch admitted to himself that he couldn't conquer all the variables by raiding storerooms at Air Force Bases. There were hundreds of necessary items the Air Force had no reason to stock, like solar panels, portable generators, freeze-dried food, field toilets and family-sized tents.

He would need to bet it all on some strategy of survival *other* than becoming frontier settlers. Setting up an entire farm, like a modern-day homesteader, wasn't going to be possible. Not now...

In a storeroom beside the armory, Dutch and Teddy found Doom and Bloom STOMP med kits, stashed away in a locker reserved for pararescue training. They rushed to the base PX and loaded up on military fatigues in their sizes: boots, socks, underwear, feminine hygiene products, and toilet paper. Dutch sped through the cosmetics section and picked up hair dye for himself and Sharon. Then he grabbed a beard trimmer, not sure if he would have electricity to even run it. In a flash of guilt, Dutch insisted on leaving his credit card with the befuddled cashier as they hurried out the door, running against the clock.

They made their last stop at the airman survival container and stocked up on compact water filters, one-man tents, knives in various sizes, flashlights, radios that Dutch didn't how to use, mace and Meals Ready to Eat.

The MREs presented a particular challenge. Dutch compared their weight with the practical limitations of airplane cargo and concluded that he had a problem. To Dutch, the meals seemed to weigh well over one pound each, and they would add up very fast.

He knew he wouldn't be abandoning Robbie Leforth, nor Janice Foster, at Offutt Air Force Base, no matter Sam Greaney's push to get rid of the chief of staff. The same would go for another half-dozen of the team aboard the plane. His new "family group" numbered around ten people, and that would add up to thirty MREs per day or at least nine hundred pounds of MREs per month. If they were stuck in the boonies for a year, they would have to pack over twenty thousand pounds of food— much more than Dutch imagined a Boeing 747-8 could carry and still get off the ground.

Dutch called ahead to the pilot and asked.

"Sir," the pilot replied, "we can carry a *hundred tons* of whatever you want. Ten tons won't be a problem." Dutch jumped behind the wheel of the Humvee and sent the supply officer to track down twenty pallets of MREs and a forklift and meet him at the plane.

As Dutch crossed the basics of survival off his hurried list, he returned to thinking about his long-term strategy. How could his family enter a fresh, belligerent world with a decisive advantage? How could he trade the next fifteen minutes for a plan that would catapult his loved ones ahead of the curve?

Dutch made a hard U-turn, bumped over the curb and onto the grass, then went back the way he had come. A Humvee going the other way slammed on his brakes to avoid a collision and gave the president a hearty middle finger out the window.

"Sorry, pal," Dutch apologized out loud. His son couldn't help but laugh at the irony of an enlisted man giving his Commander in Chief the bird.

"I'd bet he'd be horrified if he knew who you were," Teddy said.

"Maybe not today. There are a lot of Americans who'd probably love to see me crucified right now," Dutch finally spoke the truth to himself, and his son.

No matter what happened now, and no matter how much virtue and honor he had intended, he would forever be the president who presided over the greatest horror to *ever* touch the United States of America.

22

Dutch and Teddy had returned to the armory, much to the shock of the enlisted man standing behind the front counter. Two hours before, his superior officers had helped the president. Now, they were tied up at the base gate practicing riot control. The young airman would have to handle the scenario by himself. Noticing the young man's discomfiture, Dutch jumped ahead of the stress he could see painted across the young man's face.

"Feel free to take pictures with your phone so you're not held responsible for what happens next."

The young enlisted man nodded and went to work helping Dutch and Teddy demolish their stores of weapons and ammunition.

Dutch first had the young airman set aside all the firearms and ammunition he thought they might need for base defense. Then Dutch grabbed every weapon they could lay hands on, including belt-fed machine guns, links, grenades, cleaning kits, tactical flashlights and every remaining case of ammunition in the building.

The more he thought about it, the more Dutch figured that

military firearms might be worth their weight in gold. While Dutch hadn't planned well enough to own a farm or a cattle ranch, he could do the next best thing: work for a farmer or rancher to keep land and animals out of the hands of the lawless. If the civilized world failed completely, a truck full of military weapons and ammunition could probably be traded for hundreds of acres of arable land, complete with wells, herds of beef cattle, horses and farm equipment. Dutch knew it was a guess, but it was his best stab at getting ahead in a world where people no longer respected property rights. Even in that world, no sane person would walk into machine gun fire to steal a cow.

Dutch would bring the guns, and maybe the gunmen—thinking of his secret service detail—and given the right rancher or farmer, he might be able to strike a mutually-beneficial partnership.

The idea of himself cruising the countryside as a gunman made Dutch feel like a macho-fantasy fool, but he looked across the base at the smoke hanging over Omaha and he suddenly didn't feel quite so foolish.

Dutch heard the artificial click-hiss of a cell phone camera and turned to see the young airman taking snapshots of the president in front of the Humvee, now bristling with gun barrels, poking out in every direction.

"Just so they don't think I took the guns for myself," the airman explained feebly.

Dutch laughed and shook the young airman's hand. He would've loved to say something presidential in that moment, but he felt more like a pirate than a president, leaving the base security with less than half their ammunition and a small percentage of their guns. Dutch hoped they would no longer need them after he took to the air and the angry crowd disbursed.

"I hope I didn't leave you guys in a bad way," Dutch apologized, nodding toward the Humvee.

"We're good, sir. We have more cases of ammunition in a bunker on the far side of the airfield. I'll pull together a work detail and resupply the armory as soon as you leave. Don't worry about us, sir. We'll defend our base."

Dutch sighed, wondering if they really would. He doubted their fuel reserves would last more than a month, the generators running night and day. Without food shipments coming from the outside, the base would quickly burn through their stores of fresh food and MREs. While foraging on their base, Dutch estimated that Offutt had a couple hundred pallets of Meals Ready to Eat and those would disappear fast with almost 9,000 servicemen and women, plus dependents, relying upon them as their only source of food.

No matter how strong or prepared, everyone would suffer given the collapse of modern civilization. Even in the middle of Oklahoma, Dutch guessed that Offutt Air Force Base probably got half their food from Mexico and California, which might as well be on the dark side of the moon now that trucks weren't running. In a thousand ways, no one had contemplated since the Great Depression, modern man would be sucker punched over and over with critical needs they had long forgotten in the comfortable haze of global shipping and Amazon Prime.

Even the American military.

23

W hile Dutch gathered supplies, Sharon McAdams had been working through the complement and crew of Air Force One, leaving most of them at Offutt Air Base and keeping only those people absolutely necessary to a recovery of the United States. Some had resisted the idea of leaving the President's side. Others had been more than happy to get off the sinking ship. One despondent man had been driven to self-destruction already. The blood stain still hadn't been washed out of the carpet in the office section of the plane.

As the plane prepared to depart, Sharon debriefed her husband in the Oval Office.

"Sam Greaney showed up with five support men instead of the four you agreed to," Sharon said, her shoulders pitched forward in aggravation.

Dutch sighed. He would love nothing more than to kick Sam off the plane, his resignation letter in hand. The trust between the two men had taken serious hits in the last few days, and it would most likely never recover—no matter how successful they were in restitching the fabric of the nation.

But the trouble of replacing Sam at this point was far greater than the trouble of making their strained relationship work. Dutch owed it to America to put aside his annoyance with the man and to get both their backs behind the work at hand. Restoring the broken union would require the military, and nobody understood the moving parts of the military better than Sam Greaney.

"It's okay. Let it be," Dutch tried to assuage her concern, though he knew it to be futile. Sharon kept her own counsel, and if she were uncomfortable with a scenario, nothing Dutch could say would make much difference.

"Jeff Crane's wife and daughter died in a looter attack in Fairfax," Sharon reported, her eyes turning down at the corners.

Dutch closed his eyes and laid his head back against the office chair, picturing the woman and her child perishing in a state of fear and violence, not fifteen miles from the White House.

"My God, Sharon. I should've done more...the worst part: I don't even know who Jeff Crane is."

"He's the lead pilot, Dutch. He's been flying us in Air Force One for two years."

"Okay, yes. I apologize. I wasn't thinking straight. Of course, Colonel Crane. How is he holding up?"

"He's a patriot. He does what he must for his country... just like you." Sharon reached over the desk and put her hand on Dutch's. "Did you get done what you needed to do at Offutt?"

They both knew what he had been doing and they both were reluctant to say it out loud—as though thinking of their family while the country suffered was a dirty secret. "Yes, I did. Teddy and I gathered what we could. I hope we didn't leave the base short."

"It's just an insurance policy, Dutch. Now you can focus on just one thing: fixing what is broken. Right?" Sharon looked him in the eyes, still holding his hand, lending him some of her iron strength.

"Yes. Let's get to work. Did Robbie make it back aboard?"

"Of course he did. A thousand horses couldn't pull him away from your side." Sharon smiled. "I think he's a new man now that he's had a shower."

"Are we fully resupplied?" Dutch asked. In these two hours, she had become the head of the logistics team aboard Air Force One.

"Yes. They're loading the last of the pallets you sent, and then we'll be ready to take off. Can I get you anything before they make us put on our seatbelts?"

"Did the flight attendants stay with the plane?" Dutch raised his eyebrows in surprise.

"Nope. We're a skeleton crew now. We have our pilot, co-pilot, Sam Greaney and his men, our family, Robbie and Janet, and your secret service detail...I couldn't get them to stay at the airbase no matter how hard I argued."

"Men and their duty..." Dutch said, his own sense of duty inspired by the commitment of his protective detail. "Let's get America back."

24

Revived and recommitted, Dutch's team reconvened in the conference room the moment Air Force One reached cruising altitude and resumed its racetrack loop around the troubled American skies.

"First," Dutch ordered, "what's our command and control plan from here? We can't stay in the air forever. The base commander at SAC told me the network of U.S. air bases is running low on maintenance and pre-flight personnel for the refueling flights, and that they might not be capable of sustaining midair refueling much longer."

Sam Greaney stood and pointed toward the Southwestern quadrant of the map. "I've taken the liberty of sending a regiment of M1 Abrams main battle tanks from Fort Bliss to meet us at Cannon Air Force Base, about a hundred miles east of Albuquerque, New Mexico. The location is far enough away from population centers that we won't be forced to spend a lot of energy protecting our command and control base. The tanks should be more than enough protection. Also, winter won't be a problem that far south. We can dig in at Cannon and re-establish control with a maximum amount of resource and a minimum amount of friction."

"All right." Dutch pushed the meeting forward. "Please give me a report on foreign threats and enemy activity."

Sam Greaney addressed the small group seated around the conference table. "We still have no actionable intelligence that indicates any one foreign instigator over another. We're operating on the theory that the Russians launched the power grid hack, but it could've been the North Koreans or even the Chinese. The Iranians and Saudis are bludgeoning one another back to the time of Mohammed, so I really doubt either of them had grand designs on destroying the U.S."

"Is anyone approaching our territory?"

"Well," Sam rubbed his chin. "The Chinese are putting to port in a fairly heavy way, but everyone's putting their naval forces to port, given the new war in the Middle East and global instability in general. The Russians are sailing everything they have, which wasn't much anyway. I'm sure their subs are on station off the East Coast, but they would do that in any DEFCON 2 scenario. Our subs are sitting within firing range of Moscow."

"And the rest of the world?" Dutch asked.

"As expected, the Indians and Pakistanis are massing on their borders. With our forces pulling back, that was inevitable. In Europe, not surprisingly, we're seeing the same kind of civil disorder we have here. What's strange is that some of our bases in Germany and France are reporting sectarian violence from Muslim immigrants directed at Americans. It's not anything we can't handle, but it's odd that the attacks are happening in a semi-coordinated manner so quickly after the collapse of the markets. The remnants of ISIS and ISIL are being invigorated by our misfortune, it appears. And there's a level of organization I wouldn't have predicted."

"Thank you, Sam. There's not much we can do on the international front. Let's focus on getting the U.S. back on its feet. Robbie, tell me where we're at with the power grid."

"We're dead in the water, sir. It's been seven days since the cyberattack, and our entire team of NSA programmers addressing the hack is down to two guys who live at the office. I have no idea how the power companies' programming teams are holding up. They're probably gone, if I had to guess. Since two days after the attack, our programmers have been turning into ghosts—*poof*. I can't hardly blame them. Driving to work in D.C. has been tantamount to surviving Mad Max. It's not something we can reasonably ask Millennial programmers to do. Our two-week estimate for defeating the hack assumed that all teams would be working full time. We were able to maintain that level of response for about thirty hours, then people started calling in sick. Then they quit answering their phones. Sir, there is no chance we'll get the grid back up until we've restored civil order."

"That's your department, Sam." Dutch turned toward the big LCD screen. America was entirely black, the power outage universal. "I'll state the obvious: the map's not looking good."

Around the major cities the red had consumed all green—any pockets of civil order created by troops had been lost, and troops had pulled outside the big cities. The orange military markers all hovered around the areas of civil disorder.

"We've consolidated our remaining troops around the twelve largest cities, and we're cordoning them off rather than trying to stamp out civil disorder one flash point at a time. Our troop numbers have declined from over four hundred thousand to under two hundred thousand due to sky-high desertion rates, especially among married servicemen. Our troops aren't stupid —they know that without the banks there won't be paychecks. These soldiers are witnessing the worst of the civil disorder first-hand, and many of them are vanishing in the night to return to their families. Sometimes they're taking war materiel with them. But I'm highly confident that we've shaken off the strap-hangers, and now we're working with hardened men of duty, especially the officers. The remaining generals and colonels are *my guys* now, and they know how to execute orders."

"What's the plan, then?" Dutch wondered aloud. "How do troops holding *outside* the cities help us restore civil order?"

Sam Greaney pointed to Chicago where the red area of civil disorder looked like an octopus reaching inland from Lake Michigan. "For example, we have troops blockading Chicago and Milwaukee at bridges on the interstates here, here, here, and here." Greaney pointed to a dozen or more choke points along the major interstates where the red octopus suddenly stopped its reach from the inner bergs of Chicago. "It's not a perfect barrier, but we're holding in the majority and we're stopping all vehicle traffic. By setting up check points and dealing with lawless people one group at a time, we're containing the civil disorder and keeping it from spreading into the heartland."

A jolt of electricity went up Dutch's spine and his ears started to ring. "Sam...it looks like you're creating hell-holes where Americans are being sent back to die. Is *that* what I'm hearing?"

The Secretary of Defense sighed and set down his coffee mug. "Dutch. They're dying anyway. We're over a week into mass violence and hunger, particularly inside the urban areas. They're dying from violence. They're starting to die from failure of sanitation. They don't have any food. Pretty soon, they'll be dying from the cold."

"Who is *they*, Sam?" Dutch forced himself to breathe. "I notice that there aren't any troops cordoning off Salt Lake City, Denver, Phoenix, or Jacksonville."

"Those cities aren't as violent. Plus, we don't have the troops to cover them all, so I sent men where they would make the most difference."

"Sam, look who you're talking to." Dutch motioned to the others in the room. "We all know what it is we're seeing on this map. We were on the campaign trail together. These are all blue cities and blue states that you're quarantining. Who are you letting pass through your checkpoints? What kind of people?"

"My exact orders were for the commanders to let anyone through who looked like they might be an asset to the heartland of America, not a liability."

"So, the troops are profiling?" Dutch hated to say it. He had been on the opposite end of the profiling argument many times as a Republican senator and then as a Republican president. He hated being the guy who sniped at another leader for racial or economic profiling, but he couldn't find a better word to describe it.

Sam Greaney's face went red. "Mister President, do we want this country back or not? The time to quibble over equality ended a week ago. Now we're playing hardball and you and I both know that we can tell a bad guy from a good guy just by looking at him."

Dutch was struck by a cascade of doubt. Considering his secretary of defense, was he looking at a good guy or a bad guy?

"So, let me make sure I understand this." Dutch needed to get his arms around what he was hearing. The moral implications felt slippery, evasive. "Our soldiers are turning back any refugee they think is a risk of causing civil disorder and sending them into the big cities; back into the looting and rioting?"

Sam tapped his pen on the back of his hand for a long second. "We're also disarming them, so we're probably lowering the level of violence in the process."

"You're seizing firearms? From everyone?"

"Not everyone. Just the people we identify as representing a high risk of violence."

"So, you decided on your own that we would shit-can the Second Amendment. Am I following you, Sam?"

Sam fired back—a gleam in his eye—brandishing more confidence than he should considering that it was the president challenging him. "I don't think you're seeing the big picture, Dutch. This collapse isn't going to turn around tomorrow, or next week, or even next month. For this country to recover, we'll need to come back as a *different people*. The liberal Democrats wanted social justice and a class of pampered poor, now they get to live with their social engineering—and die with it." Sam Greaney's voice went husky. "People are going to die—in the millions. We can't stop that now. It's already begun. What we *can* do is decide what kind of people die and what kind of people live. It's the best we can do for America now. When it's done burning," the SecDef pointed again at the map of Chicago, "what remains of America will *all be heartland,* and we will return to something akin to 1776—a nation of good people who know how to get things done."

"It's like a political eugenics program," Robbie Leforth whispered loud enough for everyone to hear. "We're using troops to funnel liberal voters into tearing each other to pieces."

Sam Greaney thundered back. "We did not *cause* this collapse, Robbie! We're playing the hand we've been dealt by fifty years of liberal, social engineering. Let the Lefties eat their own goddamn dog food. Why should our farmers pay the price for their idiocy?"

Dutch's head swam. If it weren't for the death and violence attached to Sam's words, he might even have agreed.

Sharon knocked at the conference room door. Dutch recognized the knock and he recognized that he needed his wife's counsel to return him to true north.

"Gentlemen," Dutch said with a calm that belied the horror and magnitude of the decisions they were making. "I suggest a ten minute break. Let's reconvene at 6 p.m."

THE BLOCKADE OF CHICAGO

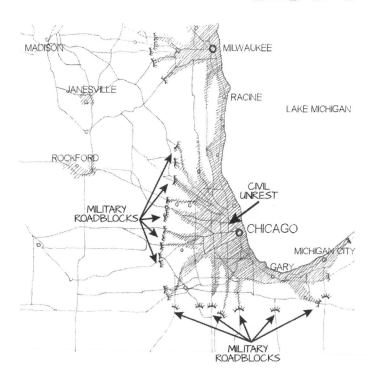

26

"Dutch. Your parents are alive," Sharon whispered as soon as she pulled her husband into their executive suite. She glanced down the hallway to make sure no one had overheard her and closed the door.

Dutch reached for the dresser and steadied himself. "I don't understand."

"Sam lied to you. I cornered one of the communications officers and convinced him that his oath was to the president and not the secretary of defense. Your parents were holed up in their ranch with their staff and neighbors when the troops checked on them. They refused to evacuate. They're probably still there, toughing it out."

"How did you know, Sharon?"

"I suspected. I didn't know."

"Why would Sam lie to me about my parents?" Dutch drilled the carpet with his eyes.

"He needed you to side-step Posse Comitatus, and he knew that you would need to be knocked off your emotional game before you would consent to something like that."

"Am I that easy to manipulate?" Dutch steadied his breathing, relief and self-doubt washing over him in alternating waves.

"Darling, we're *all* that easy to manipulate. It's just that most people don't use it as a weapon."

"They're alive..." Dutch spoke the new truth aloud. "Sharon. My folks are still alive."

Sharon pulled the President of the United States to her chest while he found balance once again.

27

President Dutch McAdams returned to the conference room with his four secret service agents in tow. He turned to Sam Greaney and in a calm voice said, "Sam, I'm putting you under arrest."

The SecDef launched to his feet. "Explain," he demanded.

"No. I won't explain. It ends here. Gentlemen, please pat him down and take him to the press section of the plane and handcuff him to a seat. We'll leave him with the MPs at our next stop."

"What are the charges?" Sam Greaney pressed while the secret service agents frisked him.

"Does it really matter at this point?" the president answered. "Treason. Lying to me about my parents. Instructing troops to violate the Constitution. I'm the one America elected. The guys with the guns are with me, not you. So, like I said, it ends right here."

"You never did figure it out," Greaney smiled as the secret servicemen handcuffed his hands behind his back. "Everyone in your administration knew it but you. You're a clown, Dutch. A political bobblehead who sounds great on camera. But you aren't capable of making the hard choices or doing the tough math. My way is best for America, but you're too soft to see it through." Greaney nodded at the darkened map.

The secret servicemen began to haul Sam Greaney out of the conference room and Dutch held up a hand.

"Tell me, Sam. Why did you have your security detail bring frangible ammo aboard my airplane? Were you planning on seizing control of the United States right from the start?"

Sam Greaney chuckled and shook his head. "You're the only person in this whole game, Dutch, who isn't thinking three moves ahead. You've been behind the curve since before you were elected. My advice Dutch, for the sake of you and your family: just let it play out. You're too late to catch up. Release me and let me do my job. It'll be better for everyone."

Dutch felt a stone in the pit of his stomach—the realization dawning that there might be much more he didn't know about Sam Greaney.

"Are you saying you planned the collapse? That you and your compatriots did this to America?"

The former secretary of defense chuckled. "Not at all, Dutch. Nobody can orchestrate something this big. The Deep State has burned to the ground along with everything else. No, Dutch; like the Russians and the Chinese and whoever else jumped on the bandwagon when this collapse kicked off, I'm just an investor staying ahead of the market. I'm watching history in the making, and I'm setting America up for long-term gain even though we're taking a beating at the moment. We'll come out of this okay, if we stick to *my* plan. I brought the frangible ammo on board in case you got stupid—maybe started listening to your wife's psychobabble. The frange was just a backup plan to the backup plan. Don't take it personally, Dutch. You can still come back from this mistake. Have your trained gorillas release me and let's get back to work. The moment we walk out of this office, it *will* be too late."

"Lock him up," Dutch ordered.

The meeting broke up as three secret servicemen pulled Sam Greaney out of the office and headed down the hallway toward the security section. Robbie turned left behind them, following the men and their prisoner toward the back of the plane. The President headed toward his stateroom, stewing on Greaney's disdain.

28

B efore Dutch had taken six steps toward his stateroom, the plane exploded in gunfire.

A ricochet buzzed down the hallway, and Dutch's secret serviceman shoved him to the floor, covering him with his body, searching for targets with his Glock. The firefight farther aft of the airplane continued. A whining howl wailed underneath the staccato bursts of handgun fire.

Dutch caught sight of Sharon, peeking through the doorway to the presidential suite.

"Get back inside. Take cover behind the dresser. Do it now!" Dutch shouted, thinking of his son and daughter, probably seated at the back of the plane.

A man thundered down the stairway from the upper level and opened fire when he saw Dutch's secret service agent. The agent returned fire, forcing the comms officer to take cover around the corner of the stairs. The handgun rounds disappeared into the walls of the airplane, doing untold damage.

Dutch's secret service agent and the assailant from the communications room screamed at one another to drop their weapons—nobody willing to back down.

A dull thud came from above. A comms officer—confederate of Sam Greaney—tumbled down the stairs, ass-over-teakettle. He sprawled limp, when he hit the floor in front of Dutch. The secret service agent shot the man in the face, then twisted to meet any new threats coming down the stairs.

"Don't shoot!" another man from the comms room stepped slowly down the stairs holding a Haliburton Zero hard-sided suitcase over his head.

"I knocked him out for you. Don't shoot. I'm one of the good guys!" The Air Force aide de camp slowly descended the steps holding the "nuclear football" high.

"Get back up there and keep control of the comms center. Take that gun," the secret service agent yelled, nodding to the dead man, apparently convinced of the aide de camp's loyalty to the president.

Dutch scrambled forward, picking up the dead man's Beretta. "We *all* fight. My children are back there." Dutch pointed toward the back of the airplane with the Beretta. He turned to the aide de camp, Captain Spilinek. "Grab a gun from the weapons locker upstairs and get your ass back down here to help."

Dutch searched the dead man and found another magazine in one of his pockets. Hugging tightly to the wall, he gained his feet and stalked down the hallway toward the now-sporadic shooting. The secret service agent pushed past him, apparently accepting Dutch's decision to fight, but unwilling to let the president take the first rounds.

The hallway narrowed and turned when they hit the conference room door. Dutch could see the lower half of a body on the ground, and nausea rose as he recognized Robbie Leforth's slacks.

The secret service agent crouched low and took a snap peak around the corner. No gunfire followed. The fight had apparently devolved into a Mexican standoff between the office section and the security section of the plane.

"Sir, our secret service team must've ducked into the office section when they started taking fire. Don't lean into the corridor. It's a fatal funnel. Someone has it covered from the rear of the plane."

"Agent Brooks," Dutch yelled around the corner. "What's your status? Do you have my children with you?"

The head of security replied. "Sir, we have Greaney and we're all three good-to-go in here. Nobody else was in this compartment. Mister Leforth is down."

"We have your kids," an unknown voice shouted from the security section at the back of the plane. "Cut Sam Greaney loose and we'll send your kids up. Straight trade. We'll give you a two-for-one, even."

Captain Spilinek, the aide de camp, armed with a handgun joined Dutch and his agent in the passageway.

The aircraft intercom blared before Dutch could reply to the gunman's demands.

29

"I don't know what's going on back there," the pilot spoke calmly over the intercom, "but my aircraft is leaking air. Whatever it is you're doing, please stop or we'll all die. I've got another hour or so of oxygen before y'all pass out."

"Just let me go, Dutch," Sam Greaney shouted from the office section. "You're not going to win this. Even if you do, I'm the only one who has a chance of pulling this mess back together. The generals on the ground are all mine—I made sure of it."

Sharon appeared behind Dutch, pressed against the wall of the hallway. Dutch considered ordering her back to the executive suite but realized she wouldn't go back while their children were in danger.

"How do you see this playing out, Sam?" Dutch yelled, buying time for his children. "Do you think you and I are going to head back to work now that your private assassins have killed Robbie? Is that what you're imagining?"

"You're not offering any solutions for the country, Dutch. I am. Let me do my job. Let's put the plane down, you get off with your people and the trinkets you picked up at SAC, we patch that hole, you give me the nuclear football and written authorization to continue operating military command. I'll fly away to do my job for the country. You stay on the ground to do your job for your family."

"There's no way in hell..." Dutch shouted but Sharon clamped her hand on his arm, interrupting him.

"Do it," she hissed into Dutch's ear. "Trust me. Give him what he wants."

Dutch swiveled on his heels and stared intently at his wife, trying to gauge her intention. Slowly, he pivoted toward the ugly negotiation, holding his country in one hand and his family in the other.

What kind of man sacrifices his family for his country?

What kind of man sacrifices his country for his family?

Dutch already knew his answers, but he paused to weigh his honor and the lives of hundreds of millions that hung in the balance.

"Trust me," Sharon repeated.

"Okay," Dutch swallowed hard before he said his next words. "I need a show of good faith, then we'll do it your way. Have your men send Abigail forward and I'll route the plane toward a contingency landing site. You'll get everything you want." *And everything you deserve,* Dutch fumed secretly, biding his time.

Sam Greaney instructed his men to let the president's daughter go.

A few minutes later Abigail dashed into the hallway and ran into the arms of her mother. The two women hurried to safer quarters at the nose of the aircraft.

Dutch nodded at the secret service agent and his aide de camp, lifted slowly out of his crouch and moved toward his office.

As he walked past Robbie Leforth's lifeless body, conviction overtook Dutch. He would dishonor Robbie's death if he handed command to Sam Greaney. So many had made the ultimate sacrifice to defend the United States of America, and now Dutch McAdams would trade it away for the life of his son. The thought caused his knees to go weak, and Dutch stepped into his office to gather his thoughts before turning Air Force One toward a landing place for his family.

Like everything else in life, this crossroads wasn't simple. The nation Dutch had been elected to lead had made its choice —it had decided to abandon the Rule of Law. Dutch knew he was placing blame on hungry, desperate people, but in the end, they were voters, not blundering cattle. They chose to end their government, and many would die with that choice on their breath.

Dutch hadn't been elected to force people into doing the right thing or even the smart thing. By rioting and rejecting the leadership of the United States government, the people had effectively impeached him and every other elected official. Of course, not everyone had made the choice to loot and riot, but enough had chosen lawlessness that the military hadn't been able to put the genie back in the bottle. The inner-city populations had voted with their feet, plain and simple.

This train of thought brought Dutch back to Sam Greaney's brutal plan. Was locking inner city rioters into their self-made hell really such a bad idea? Preserving the heartland for capable survivors made a lot of sense, at least on paper.

And that was the rub. Dutch had seen it more times than he could count: policies that looked good on paper that resulted in incalculable evil. Dutch had long ago learned that a decision not only had to look good on paper, but it had to pass the smell test.

Greaney's plan smelled foul to the president. Dutch could describe his disagreement in twenty ways, but it all boiled down to the reality that his soul could not abide it.

But Dutch wasn't going to sacrifice his son to hold that line. He would find another way.

30

A lone in his office, Dutch settled on Mountain Home, Idaho as their landing place. More than forty miles from Boise and almost three hundred miles from Salt Lake City, the spartan, Cold War strategic bomber base would give the first family a remote location to put down, far from inquisitive eyes and angry mobs. More importantly, the plane could reach Mountain Home before they all died of hypoxia.

The satellite feed on Dutch's laptop showed southern Idaho to be an area between farms and sprawling, gray swaths of desert. It looked like a place he could hide his face and rebuild the government. Southern Idaho would be their last stand, both as a family and as a presidency. Dutch picked up his phone and played the last chip in his stack.

"Captain Spilinek," Dutch said to his aide de camp, now running the comms center. "Please call ahead to Mountain Home Air Force Base and let them know we have a priority landing coming their way in about two hours. Tell them it's a Code Raptor-300 event and request that three Strykers mobilize out of Boise with minimal crew, all single males, to meet us at Mountain Home. Do you copy the last?"

"Yessir. Radio Mountain Home AFB, let them know a Code Raptor-300 event is coming in one-two-zero minutes and to scramble three Strykers out of the armory in Boise with a skeleton crew, fully-equipped, all single males, to meet us at the airfield."

"Correct. And, Captain," the president said, "do not tell them we're Air Force One or that the first family is aboard. You got that? Please let the pilot know to change course."

"Roger, sir."

Dutch hung up the phone, closed his laptop and headed into the presidential suite to check on his wife and daughter.

Both women were sitting on the edge of the bed talking when Dutch entered. Abigail had been crying.

"We're heading toward southern Idaho, and we'll land in about two hours. What do you think?"

Sharon nodded approval.

"Abigail was just telling me that Sam Greaney's men had been preparing to take over the plane since we left Offutt. They had Abby and Teddy restrained in the security section, waiting for the signal from Greaney."

It made sense. The new men Greaney traded out for his Delta security detail must've been plants who'd been on the airplane since D.C., probably sitting in the back posing as staff. That meant Sam had at least seven combat operators on board when they took off. The men must have been standing by since before the California nuke. There would be no other way Sam could've had them ready in time to board the plane.

"It makes me wonder if we were the only ones that didn't see this collapse coming," Dutch said. "How could Sam have known the threat was so serious?" He scratched his head.

Sharon thought about it. "We were hearing it on the news a few times a week for the last couple years. I couldn't watch the news without seeing some kind of doomsday scenario: climate catastrophes, credit bubbles, solar flares, volcanos, flu and EMP threats from rogue nations." She shrugged. "Maybe Sam Greaney was just playing the odds. He wasn't picking up the tab for having a team of commandos standing at the ready. Why not invest in any possible outcome? Sam Greaney's not the kind of man who would ever stand by and be happy with your successes, Dutch. I'm sure he always saw himself as the rightful leader of the country... the sociopathic, paranoid bastard."

The hammering of gunfire echoed down the plane's fuse-lage. Dutch motioned for his wife and daughter to stay behind the furniture, and he rushed down the hallway, drawing his handgun from the back of his belt and pulling up short at the cover provided by the bulge of the conference room. The shooting stopped. An eerie quiet descended over Air Force One, broken only by the whine of the engines and the whistle of air escaping through bullet holes.

31

"Report, Agent Brooks," Dutch called around the corner.

"We're all good here, sir. They just had a shootout back in the security section. From the sound of it, I believe one of the Army operators had a bone to pick regarding their loyalties and he dropped the hammer on his buddies."

"Teddy," Dutch yelled. "Are you okay back there."

"He's fine," one of the operators yelled from the rear compartment. Someone muffled Teddy's shouts, probably gagging him. "We've got things under control. Stay out of this section or the kid dies."

Dutch rounded the corner and darted into the office staff section. His four secret servicemen crouched behind a desk that they had propped up as a barricade. Sam Greaney sat handcuffed to a chair in the corner, a blank look on his face.

"My moneys on someone having died back there, Mister President. Maybe more than one. Should we consider rushing them, sir?"

"Do we have a solid count?" Dutch asked.

"We did before the shooting," one of the agents—Dutch

didn't know his name—answered. "There were four men, plus the one we killed on the staircase. Now it could be less. But we could be walking into an even gunfight. And they're posted up on the hallway. We have to assume they're some kind of SOF guys, maybe Delta. Maybe former SEALs. Even with only two operators back there, and even if they didn't have a hostage, the odds wouldn't be good."

"Hold position," Dutch ordered. "We play this out for more time. Has anyone checked on the hole in the plane?"

"I found it. It's in the outside wall of the staff office," the lead agent, Brooks, answered. "One of the nine millimeter rounds hit a seam in the aluminum and punched straight through. I tried to plug the hole with a plastic patch and it might've helped. But we can still hear the pressure escaping around the patch. The pilot says we can lose pressure like this for maybe an hour before we go hypoxic—maybe twice that if the pilot flies lower. After that, we'll need to wear the O2 masks. If the bullet had blown out a window...that would've been a different story."

"Someone moved Robbie's body," Dutch noted, his voice heavy.

"We moved he and the dead comms guy into the staff office until we can offload them."

"Gentlemen," a quiet voice interrupted. The Air Force aide de camp motioned for them to come forward on the plane. "Can I show you something?"

Dutch and the lead agent, Brooks, slipped around the dogleg in the hallway and quietly followed the young Air Force officer upstairs to the comms center.

The three men filed up the narrow staircase and entered a room packed with computer monitors. A few 1980s-era radio sets still held a place on the wall, but almost everything else had been converted into computerized communication transceivers. A door opened at the far end of the comms center and Sharon stepped through from the nose of the plane, the flight deck and the pilots behind her.

Just like Sharon, Dutch mused. *Checking on everyone to make sure their needs are being met.* She slipped past them while touching Dutch's arm, and headed down the staircase.

"After the shooting, I poked around the wifi network on the plane and found not one, but two computers still on the network. Both the screens, fore and aft, in the security and passenger compartments aren't actually television screens. They're computer monitors. Somebody probably wanted to have more flexibility for presentations, so they installed full monitors. Check it out. That means they have built-in cameras."

The young officer hit the return key and a rear-facing view of the aft security compartment appeared. Both Dutch and Agent Brooks leaned forward, gobbling up the new information.

"There's only two of them," Brooks pointed out. "See that foot on the floor," he nodded toward a boot poking around a row of airplane seats. "That's a dead man. Have you seen anyone but these two guys and the hostage?"

"I was only watching them for a minute before I went to get you, so I can't be sure there isn't another guy hiding out somewhere. He could be in the john."

"There's Teddy," Dutch touched the screen. The back of his son's head with his flyaway blond hair poked above a seat. "He's in a back row, facing away."

"Here," the aide de camp hit another key and the view toggled to a head-on shot of Teddy, bound and gagged. "This is the other computer monitor and it's facing the opposite direction."

Other than appearing uncomfortable, Teddy seemed fine.

"Okay, gentlemen." Dutch stood back and folded his arms. "How do we use this information to keep our nation out of the hands of a psychopath?"

32

"Sir. When you loaded the supplies from Offutt, did you requisition any M84 grenades?" Agent Brooks asked, excitement mounting in his voice.

"I have no idea what I grabbed. Are you former military, Agent Brooks?"

"MARSOC Marine, sir. An M84 is a flashbang grenade—it looks like a V8 juice can with a big handle, a ring and a bunch of holes drilled in the sides."

Dutch remembered the scene at the Air Force armory. "I recall a bunch of little baseball-looking grenades and then some skinny grenades with holes."

"We can't use the fragmentation grenades—the ones like baseballs. The overpressure and frag would compromise the hull of the aircraft. I'm pretty sure the flashbang won't hurt the plane, though."

"Don't we want a grenade to cause damage?" Dutch asked.

"Yeah, but not so much that it'll kill your boy or split a seam in the aircraft. And if those guys are Delta, or anything in that family of operator, we'll need to do more than flashbang them to put them back on their heels. Those men will be dedicated adversaries. First things first. Did they load the grenades in the forward compartment or the rear?"

"I'm not sure. I think the food pallets got forklifted into the back. I'm guessing they loaded the other stuff up front to balance the load."

"Good. The forward lower compartment is right down the stairs up front. Let me check to see if the grenades are up front where I can get at them. Maybe Jesus is smiling on us after all. How much time do we have?" the agent looked at his watch.

Dutch looked at his own watch and did the math. "I have to check with the pilot, but I think we're about ninety minutes out from Mountain Home, which means we might be sucking thin air before then, depending on how good your patch worked. Best guess: we'll be on the edge of passing out in less than an hour."

"Why don't we just wait until they pass out and then get Teddy?" the aide de camp offered.

"We don't have mobile O2 units on this aircraft. If they pass out, we pass out. If we have O2 masks, they have O2 masks. We can breathe through our little masks hanging from the ceiling, but then we're in no position to assault. They'd be breathing off their ceiling O2 masks and shooting from fixed positions. We're the ones who need to be mobile. Not them."

Everyone nodded, thinking through their complicated reality; fighting aboard an aircraft at 30,000 feet against trained commandos with a hostage. All that and they had a whistling clock ticking away their air.

Agent Brooks broke the reverie. "First things first. If we can get a couple M84s, we might have options. Meet up in the Oval Office in ten."

33

Agent Brooks thunked down two grenades on the President's desk. "We're in business. We need to find something we can use to generate light fragmentation. Sixteen penny nails would be perfect."

"I doubt there are any nails on the airplane, but I have a whole case of stainless steel Monte Blanc pens that we give away when we sign treaties." Dutch stood, dug around in his credenza and came back with a cardboard box full of gleaming, steel pens.

"Perfect," Agent Brooks grabbed one and twisted it into two metal tubes, dropping the ink insert back into the box. "We can tape a hundred of these around the grenades and they might act like flechettes. I think they'll stick into anything and everything, including the operators. The airframe should be fine."

"I didn't think an airplane could tolerate the pressure from a grenade." Dutch vaguely remembered something about a terrorist with a little bit of C-4 explosive in his shoe posing a serious threat to an airliner.

Brooks shook his head. "Air Force One is actually designed to withstand the M-84 flashbang. We bring them aboard when we have dodgy foreign nationals in the press section. There are four times as many overpressure valves on this 747 as on commercial models. We're good. Also, I found more nine millimeter frangible ammo in the weapons locker left over from the last time we flew with Saudis aboard. Even frange can damage the hull and the electronics, but it's better than shooting ball ammo."

"How do we protect Teddy from getting hit?" Dutch looked at the camera's view, Teddy's head poking over the seat back.

"Your son studied French, right?" the aide de camp said. "I've started rotating photos of France from my iPhone on both screens, just like screen savers. I think they fell for it. The commandos haven't paid any attention to the monitors. We're so accustomed to screen savers, it's not something we notice anymore." The young officer smiled at his mental victory over the trained operators. "I can start running random phrases in French and then slip in a few warnings. If we can get your son to duck and cover when the grenades fly, he should be fine."

"Look." The young officer pointed to the screen as he flipped back to the rear monitor. "Teddy is paying attention to the screen saver." The monitor showed Teddy looking directly at the camera, eyes wide.

"Do you know French?" Dutch asked.

"My family is Quebecois," the young officer said and smiled.

Agent Brooks pointed at the rows of chairs behind Teddy. "The flechettes shouldn't penetrate more than two rows of airplane seats, at most. Teddy's four rows back. If he gets his head down, I don't see how he'd get hit." The agent held up his hands. "But, it's your call, sir."

Dutch considered his conflicting obligations: his country. His family. His son. Fathers across this once-great nation were watching their children starve. At least Dutch's and Teddy's risk might make a difference.

"Let's do it," he decided, leaving the outcome to fate.

"Sir, one more thing." Agent Brooks cringed. "I'll be going in first on the assault, and I'd like to use Secretary Greaney as a human shield. I know that probably offends your sense of honor, but those operators will think twice before they shoot their boss. At least I hope they'll think twice—"

Dutch interrupted him. "—Fuck that guy. Pardon my French. He's holding my son hostage. Cut off his head and stick it on a pole if you think it'll help."

34

L*es grenades arrivent bientôt...Préparez-vous à vous couvrir la tête.*

President McAdams, Agent Brooks and the Air Force aide de camp watched the words appear on the screen, then disappear. Teddy nodded emphatically into the camera, now fully aware of the scheme.

"They didn't notice the text," the young man rubbed his hands together. "They should've spent more time studying in high school, less time lifting weights."

"They're getting lax," Agent Brooks observed. "They've been on-point for over an hour and they're letting down a bit— assuming that we won't come at them while they have a hostage. If we pitch the flashbangs just past the first row of seats, they should get a face full of stainless steel."

"Is there any reason not to go right now?" Dutch asked.

"Yes, we *should* go now, but you misunderstand, Mister President. Under no circumstance will I allow *you* to participate in this assault." Agent Brooks set his feet.

"Tell you what, Agent Brooks," Dutch switched into negotiation mode. "I'll be your backup if things go sideways. I'll hang back in the office section unless I'm needed. That's my final offer," Dutch held up the Beretta to prove to the secret service agent that he was going in one way or the other. The agent would to have to wrestle the gun away from the president to stop him.

"Okay, then it's five of us going in, the President in reserve and the secretary of defense out front. This should work," Agent Brooks said.

At sixty-three years old, it had been almost fifty years since Dutch had been in a physical confrontation with another man. Even so, he remembered those schoolyard brawls and he wondered how he would respond to combat in the real world, with real bullets. With combat looming, Dutch had to ask, *am I a coward?*

Once, when Dutch had been walking his girlfriend home from middle school, her books in his arms, an older boy from high school confronted them on the sidewalk, smacked the books to the ground and taunted Dutch with insults against the girl's maidenhood. Dutch feigned helplessness. Since the high school boy had fifty pounds and three inches of reach on him, acting helpless made sense. But in that moment, Dutch's mind worked out a plan to inflict maximum damage on the bigger boy.

Dutch acted as though he was turning away, and then he'd loaded every pound of force he could into his hips, and let loose the biggest haymaker of his life, directly into the center of the bigger boy's face.

The high school boy had gone down hard on the sidewalk.

The boy had looked up at Dutch and his girlfriend, swiped away the blood gushing from his nose and said, "Now, I'm going to beat the shit out of you."

Dutch had been too astonished at the success of his gambit

to realize that he should've set to kicking the boy as soon as he'd hit the ground. Instead, he'd let him get up.

Just then a police car had rolled up to the curb and a sheriff's deputy jumped out to break up the fight. Noticing the obvious size difference between the boys, and looking back and forth at the gushing blood coming from the high school boy's face, the officer had fist-bumped Dutch on the shoulder.

"Nice job. Now get the hell out of here and quit fighting."

To this day, Dutch didn't know for sure if he had it in him to stomp a man on the ground. He yearned to know what he would do to win back his son, or to fulfill his duty to his country.

Dutch slide-checked the breach on his Beretta, already knowing there was a round in the chamber. He looked at the video screen one last time.

"Let's get this done."

35

A gent Brooks gagged the secretary of defense. The secret service agent had a death grip on the SecDef's belt in his left hand, his Glock in his right. Behind him, another secret service agent held the two taped and bulging flashbangs, one in each hand. Behind him, the other two agents had their Glocks at the high ready. Looking rather small by comparison, the president's aide de camp held a revolver, standing last in line. Everyone, including Sam Greaney, wore body armor.

The president stood a couple paces back, pretending to hold in reserve. Not for a moment did Dutch contemplate staying there, but if it made Agent Brooks feel better, he would happily act as though he'd be avoiding the fight.

Agent Brooks didn't wait for permission.

"Go, go, go," he hissed.

The stack of men, the president at the rear, flowed into the hallway, charging toward the security section of Air Force One. Only later would Dutch piece together the cobra-fast sequence of events.

He never saw the grenades being thrown, but Dutch heard the enemy operators shout, "*Grenade!*"

Agent Brooks pushed into the entryway and crouched behind the secretary of defense. The thunder and flash overwhelmed Dutch's senses, even at the back of the line. How could men be standing up to the gut-twisting overpressure of the explosion?

But the enemy operators were fazed for only a split-second. They poured gunfire down the hallway, shooting expertly around Greaney.

Agent Brooks returned fire and the second agent in line drew his handgun and joined the fight. The four men pushed into the room, firing at the operators, shooting in and around the airline seats.

Dutch's aide de camp fell back onto him and looked up, a gout of blood pulsing from his throat. Something clicked in Dutch, like a door slamming on a section of his mind. He recognized the mortal wound and dropped the man to the floor, pushing forward, hunting to bring his own gun to bear.

One of the secret servicemen dropped, clutching his chest, and Dutch filled the gap, dumping round after round into the men behind the seats, doing his best to pull his rounds away from where his son would be hiding.

Dutch's weapon sights were the furthest thing from his mind. He mashed the trigger over and over, seeing the bloody faces of the enemy operators bobbing above and around the airplane seats, chunks of flesh apparently blown off by the grenade, but doing nothing to slow their commitment to combat.

Sam Greaney mule-kicked Agent Brooks and launched himself onto the floor toward the security section, landing face-first and clearing the hallway for his men to shoot unrestricted.

Agent Brooks took several rounds to the chest and Dutch

saw one splash off the man's shoulder, splattering Dutch's face with blood.

"Back, back, back!!" Brooks screamed as he dropped the magazine out of his Glock, rammed another one home and resumed firing.

Dutch was the first to duck around the corner back into the office section, bullets whizzing into the plastic and aluminum surfaces of the plane. Miraculously, all four secret service agents followed. Three were bleeding from extremity wounds, one had been grazed across the head and all of them had been shot in the body armor. Dutch was the only man to escape unscathed.

"Mother fucker, those bastards are tough," one of the secret service agents wheezed, likely suffering from broken ribs. The five men gulped air and coughed, alive but defeated. The truth of their failure soon eclipsed the rush of adrenaline.

Dutch's son remained in the hands of ruthless killers.

36

The firefight had further damaged the airframe, and the whistling from the hull could be heard coming from several locations. Dutch didn't need to ask the pilot; he knew they would be landing or losing consciousness soon. During the fight, the oxygen masks had popped out of the ceilings.

"Dutch," the secretary of defense called out, now together with his commandos in the security section. Greaney didn't even sound injured. "I respect the effort, but now I've got to do some things I would've rather avoided."

"Is Teddy okay?" Dutch ignored the threats.

"Oh, he's fine, but he won't be."

Teddy began to scream, then the pitch of his scream climbed to an animal shriek. Dutch launched forward into the corridor, a blind lunge toward his son. One of the secret service agents hooked Dutch's arm and wrestled him back from the shooting lane. He pinned Dutch in an iron wrestler's hold while the young man passed through his chorus of agony. Teddy's shrieking abated, and Dutch let out a choked sobbed, impossibly relieved to hear him weeping rather than silenced.

Something sailed into the office section and thunked to the ground in front of Dutch. His brain struggled to place the bloody mass until his mind reluctantly recognized a trim fingernail and he surrendered his denial. His son's severed finger leaked blood on the beige carpet of the airplane. Dutch's eyes lost focus and the bile burned in his stomach.

A finger. His son's finger. Maimed forever. But alive. Still alive.

"I'm sorry, Dutch, but pieces of your son will keep coming if you don't put this plane on the ground and give me the launch codes and your authorization to act as Commander and Chief. We're done playing."

In five minutes time, Dutch had learned two things about himself.

One; that he was no coward in a fight.

Two; that all it took to evaporate his will was his son's severed finger.

As Teddy cried in the background, and as the airframe of Air Force One warbled its death wail, Dutch McAdams surrendered the presidency to a man nobody would've ever elected.

"Okay, Sam. You win. I'm getting you the codes."

37

P*lease take your seats and buckle your seat belts. We're on final approach,* the pilot warned over the intercom.

Considering the five dead bodies, uncountable flesh wounds and Dutch's tortured son in the security section, the safety warnings sounded like a cruel joke. *Procedure will be procedure,* Dutch supposed, his mind drifting on the come-down tide of adrenaline.

Even so, Dutch sat in his office chair and buckled his seat belt.

He wondered if Sam Greaney would try to seize the airplane before they could offload. Dutch still had his secret service detail, so the two teams of fighting men would still probably cancel one another out. His men were all severely wounded, and he had no doubt the commandos were injured as well. Dutch doubted that anyone wanted another gunfight.

At this point, the variables of the situation were spread all over the map. Sam Greaney had been right: Dutch had never been good at looking three steps ahead. He had already handed the nuclear football over to Sam, but he refused to give him the combination to the suitcase locks. Also, Dutch withheld the letter of authorization, holding it until his family and supplies were off the plane.

It was the best he could do.

Dutch felt his defeat, whole and unmistakable. He knew he was handing the remnants of America over to a soulless tyrant.

The aircraft trembled as the wheels contacted asphalt. Dutch inhaled, subconsciously allowing himself to breathe again. He looked out at endless sage and rolling hills racing past his window. The Idaho desolation was to be their new home, and if the handoff went according to plan, the desolation might be their savior.

He unbuckled his seat and headed out of his office to shepherd Sharon and Abigail down the jetway, hungry to get as much of his family off the plane as he could.

The women had gathered up the most rugged clothes they could find, even while Teddy sat bleeding and maimed in the back of the plane. Everyone had to do what they could to survive. Something about that refrain struck Dutch as a new and permanent reality.

Get used to it, he told himself. He watched his wife and daughter descend the built-in jetway on Air Force One. They stepped down and greeted the soldiers—wide-eyed and gawking at the unexpected arrival of the president's airplane. The three armored vehicles he requested and two Humvees awaited.

Dutch moved aft toward the no man's land between the office section and the security section of the airplane. Sam Greaney and his commandos hid in their section, giving Dutch no idea as to their disposition. For all he knew, the operators could've died from their wounds.

"Sam, we're disembarking and unloading our gear. Send Teddy out now."

Unseen behind the bulkhead, Sam Greaney shouted back. "With respect, sir. Fuck you. You'll get him when I get my letter and the combination to the briefcase. Don't toy with me or I'll send you the middle finger. Literally. Also, get those airmen refueling us and patching the holes. You're lucky I'm even going let you have your prepper crap. I don't have to do that, you know."

Sharon must have handled offloading logistics with the airbase because Dutch heard the sound of forklifts and felt the airframe vibrate as the cargo doors opened.

"I'm going to make sure the mechanics are en route. My men will stay right here," Dutch threatened. He didn't want Greaney to get the idea that he held all the cards. Agent Brooks, still bleeding from the open wound on his shoulder, gave Dutch a thumbs up.

"Dutch. If you want your boy back with his hands still attached, you'll stay here. I don't want you going anywhere. And throw us the big med kit. Do it in the next ten minutes, or I'm going to have them cut off his right hand," Greaney demanded.

It was an unnecessary threat, but Sam Greaney apparently enjoyed making them. As he picked up the phone on the wall, Dutch couldn't imagine how he had overlooked the malignant soul in his pick for secretary of defense.

38

Air Force One taxied away moments after Dutch McAdams descended the stairs, holding Teddy up as his son stumbled down the jetway. All their supplies had been forklifted down, the holes in the airframe hastily patched, and medical supplies thrown to Sam Greaney and his hired shooters. The exchange was done, but Dutch hadn't surrendered.

Dutch had given Greaney the letter and the combination to the nuclear suitcase in exchange for his boy, but he had promised himself he would destroy the plane before he would let Sam Greaney get away.

"Did you tell them to shoot it down?" Dutch yelled at Sharon as he passed Teddy off to an Air Force medic and ran toward the armored vehicles. When Sharon replied with a bewildered look, Dutch veered toward the nearest Stryker.

"Destroy that plane *now*," Dutch shouted. The reservists stumbled about the vehicle looking for some kind of command authorization. "I'm your Commander and Chief," Dutch roared. "You don't need to confirm my order. Shoot it down!"

The crew commander finally grasped the order and

bellowed at a crewman to bring up ammo for the fifty cal. While the men struggled to load the huge machine gun on top of the Stryker, Air Force One thundered past on the opposite runway, taking to the sky just as the top plate on the machine gun slammed shut.

The Browning M2 exploded to life, the line of tracers lagging a hundred yards behind the plane as it banked off the runway. The machine gunner corrected, firing a string that chased the 747 but fell short and to the outside of its banking turn. The machine gunner elevated his next burst and placed the glowing rope exactly where the jet liner had been moments before, still falling behind.

The belt expended, the assistant gunner quickly laid another belt into the feed tray and slapped the top plate closed. Air Force One continued to climb, now almost two miles away. The machine gunner continued firing, trying to walk the line of tracers into a target approaching a speed of three hundred miles an hour. If he scored any hits, it had no apparent effect on the aircraft.

When the massive din from the machine gun died, the machine gunner apologized. "I'm sorry sir. That was my first time shooting at an aircraft. I'm sorry. I've never attempted anything like this."

Sharon stepped beside her husband as he ran his fingers through his silver hair over and over again. "Oh my God, Sharon. I let him get away with the codes. Oh my God..."

She took his hand in both of hers, calming him. "Dutch. It's going to be okay."

A familiar face stepped out from behind the Stryker and Dutch took a second to recognize the co-pilot from Air Force One. Dutch turned to his wife, struggling to understand.

Sharon looked at him with hard eyes, sadness and resolve playing across her face.

It had been the same expression a year earlier, when she had urged him to fire his secretary of state. With those same eyes, she looked toward the horizon—toward the dwindling shape of Air Force One.

"Jeff said he'd be willing to make the sacrifice if it came to that," Sharon explained without taking her eyes off the aircraft. "Jeff's wife and daughter are gone, so dying for his country would be a gift, he said."

Dutch watched the plane make a slow banking turn, then it tipped nose forward and banked in the opposite direction.

"Not everyone in this country has forgotten about honor," Sharon spoke the pilot's epithet.

Air Force One angled from the sky at full speed, then suddenly disappeared into the side of a mountain, a mile-wide starburst erupting from the grey rock. A massive, silent fireball rolled into the sky. Twenty seconds later, the sound of ripping thunder reached the airfield.

"Sweet Mary, Mother of God," Dutch whispered.

"He said it'd be a gift," Sharon turned toward Dutch and leaned her forehead against the side of his head, her tears trickling down his sideburn. "We aren't the kind of people who let a monster hold America in his hand, and neither was Jeff Crane. That wouldn't be something we could live with."

"This was you?" Dutch pleaded with her for understanding.

"Jeff...the pilot. He and I agreed that this would be best, if it came to that."

She had always been the knife's edge in their partnership—the carbon steel to his hickory grip. While Dutch struggled to think three moves ahead, Sharon did it in her sleep.

"May God have mercy on their souls," Dutch intoned, the finality of their struggle finally dawning on him.

EPILOGUE

Within hours of the death of Air Force One, a new struggle unfolded—primal, ruthless and never-ending. If ever he forgot the brutality of their new life, Dutch had only to look at his son and the stump of his left pinky finger. Gone was the boy who studied French and loved video games. His son had learned the lessons Dutch wanted him to learn, but those lessons had come at a horrific cost—evaporating the twinkle in the boy's eye and hurdling him into the calloused manhood he would likely need to survive.

Several weeks had passed and winter closed in on southern Idaho. Fleeing from the dangers of civilization, their caravan of three Strykers and three Humvees struck deep into the gray shale deserts of Idaho and Nevada, seeking refuge as far from human habitation as possible. In the end, it was the Shoshone-Paiute Indians of the Duck Valley Indian Reservation who took them in. Despite their deeply troubled history with the United States, the Shoshone-Paiutes graciously offered a home to the U.S. government *in absentia*, giving the president and his people medical care for their wounds, fresh food and above all else, secrecy.

Three miles outside of town, wedged between a reservoir and a mountainside, the McAdams family, their secret service detail and twenty-five young men from Mountain Home Air Force Base and the Idaho National Guard set up a heavily-armed garrison; protecting themselves and defending the entryway to the tiny Native American town of Owyhee, Nevada. Their ability to crush marauding gangs with high-tech weaponry more than made up for the nuisance of having strange, white faces in town.

The McAdams and their team set out into the wilderness with two communications specialists from Mountain Home, together with their SINCGARS Humvee. The communications men joined the president's entourage in order to monitor events, and perhaps someday to reconnect with fragments of the government and military. For now, Dutch didn't think he had anything to say to the military commanders in the field that they couldn't come up with on their own.

As Dutch McAdams sat atop a Stryker armored vehicle, performing his turn on guard duty, Sharon joined him. Dutch pulled her close and wrapped his heavy parka around them both, steeling them against the snowstorm building on the northern horizon.

"It's beautiful," Dutch said. "I'd forgotten how majestic it is to live outdoors."

Sharon smiled. "I might enjoy the majesty of it more when I finally forget what a hot shower feels like. I'm still grieving what was."

"Our family made it, Sharon. We're incredibly blessed."

"Except Robbie," she corrected. They sat in silence for a moment, remembering their friend.

"I spend a lot of time thinking about what I could've done differently to change things. Maybe if I hadn't called troops into the cities the riots would've burned out and food shipments would've resumed. Maybe if I'd never appointed Sam Greaney in the first place things might've ended a lot better."

"I've been thinking about it too, Dutch." Sharon regarded the coming snow flurry. "No civilization ever lasted forever. Sooner or later, every great civilization convinces itself that it's entitled to *more*. When human selfishness exceeds our ability to care for others, we reap the whirlwind... We call forth the storm. Dutch, it didn't just happen. *We* called it up. No president was ever going to stop that."

Dutch thought back to the expression on her face as she watched the fiery death of Sam Greaney and his commandos—an execution she had arranged. That memory struggled to exist in the same universe as the graceful woman sitting beside him, her cold-dappled cheeks flushing red in the winter wind.

The first, fat snowflakes settled on Dutch and Sharon, blown from the storm, traveling probably five miles before making landfall.

"Time for you to get indoors," Dutch unwrapped his parka from around her shoulder.

"What's one more squall?" She chuckled and pulled his parka back around herself. "They come, and then they go. You and I, and hopefully our kids—we're the kind of family who steps *into* the storm."

SNEAK PREVIEW

BLACK AUTUMN

The 380 page companion novel to
The Last Air Force One

available now on Amazon

Prologue:

Santa Catalina Island, California
Near Avalon Bay
Two Weeks Before the Black Autumn Collapse

After four months of living with a nuclear bomb in the hold of their sailboat, even the Koran's promise of seventy-two bare-breasted virgins wore a little thin. When they had left the Sulu Archipelago of the Philippines, dying in an atomic flash sounded like a small price to pay for even one virgin, much less six dozen. Now, with the end near at hand, the unspoken truth between the two Filipino villagers was that neither of them felt particularly eager to die.

They had decided to wait for a sign from Allah before completing the last twenty-six miles of the voyage to America. The two villagers, far from home, anchored on the east side of Catalina Island, just a handful of hours from the bustling coast of Los Angeles, California.

They had been loitering there for nearly two months and, amazingly, nobody had so much as spoken to them.

Njay and Miguel had settled into a daily routine. *Wake up. Defecate off the side of the boat. Make tea. Defecate off the side of the boat. Fish all morning. Nap. Fish all afternoon. Defecate. Eat fish. Sleep.*

The journey from the Philippines had gone exactly as planned, which amounted to a miracle in sailing. Nothing ever went exactly as planned. The well-provisioned sailboat had contributed to their successful journey. Neither of the men had ever sailed in a boat so well stocked. The boat even came with a desalinization filter sufficient for a couple months. With such a fine craft, they had been able to set a simple tack into the north-northeast trade winds directly at the coast of California. For fifty-eight days, they had kept the boat pointed on a steady course, barely having to trim the sails. It had been the easiest sailing of Njay's life.

But time was running out. Both men felt sick. They suspected the desalinization filter had worn out and was letting a small amount of salt into their drinking water. The other possibility was that the crate-sized nuclear bomb in their hold leaked radiation.

Their village imam had given Miguel and Njay simple instructions, but Njay suspected the instructions had come from the light-haired, tall man who had been skulking around their village for months. Everyone seemed to know that gossiping about Tall Man would be a violation of obedience to the imam. Njay concluded that the man must be Middle Eastern or Russian, given the nature of their mission. No Pacific Rim nation would risk war with America.

In truth, Njay knew little of the world outside his island chain, but he'd been taught much about America, with their Special Forces murderers and their weapons of unimaginable power. The United States lorded over the Pacific, threatening to blow their enemies back to the Stone Age. Like a disease consuming the hearts of man, America plagued the world, and Islam would cure it. Such a plague could be stopped by the tiniest of medicines: one small boat and two small men would vaporize the Hollywood movie stars and shake the Wall Street skyscrapers. In Allah's wise path, giants were often felled by pebbles.

The two Filipinos talked about sailing into Avalon Bay for another desalination filter, but the risk of being discovered, especially considering their almost non-existent English, was too great.

Njay and Miguel spoke endlessly about God's will while crossing the ocean and then fishing off the coast of Catalina. Would Allah really want them to sacrifice their lives if it wasn't necessary?

Based on their time in Catalina, it didn't seem like Americans worried much about the coming and going of sailboats in their waters. After four months, the two men had received nothing more than hearty waves from other boaters. Perhaps they could sail into Long Beach Harbor, tie up their sailboat, set the bomb to explode, then walk into America. Surely there were other Filipino Muslims in America who would shelter them.

They even discussed how to build a time delay for the bomb. They pulled the crate below decks apart, only to find that the bomb was a steel box with a single green button. The box had been welded shut, and the men hadn't brought any tools capable of cutting steel. The button protruded through the metal box and through the slats in the crate. Their instructions had been simple: sail into Long Beach Harbor and press the button.

A time delay device—the candle could burn through the rope and release the hammer to swing into the button. The contraption could give them a few minutes to get clear of the bomb. If they ran, they might make it.

They didn't know how big the explosion would be, nor did they know if a hammer strike would sufficiently depress the button without breaking it. Of course, it couldn't be tested in advance.

The men eventually set their time delay idea aside and put the decision in the hands of Allah. They listened to American radio as they fished, talking into the evening about how a sign from Allah might appear.

The sickness had them both concerned. Their daily defecations into the ocean were audible from everywhere on the boat, and they agreed the sickness was worsening, compelling them to relieve themselves more often.

Time grew short.

Mongratay Province, Afghanistan
Two Weeks Ago

Jeff Kirkham's adrenaline spiked before he even knew why, his subconscious recognizing the blue-white trail of a rocket propelled grenade as it whistled into his column of trucks. The low growl of a PKM machine gun and a swarm of AK-47s joined the chorus as the battlefield roared to life.

This had been the wrong place to drop overwatch, and it had been Jeff's bad call. He rocked forward, squinting through the filthy windshield, hoping he wasn't seeing what he was seeing.

Some of his best men were in the Corolla, still the lead vehicle, and they were hanging way out in the wind.

Jeff rode in the passenger seat of the command truck toward the back of the column with his shorty AK wedged between his butt and the door. Only the medical truck lagged behind them.

Endless hours of experience and training kicked in, and Jeff launched from his seat, slamming the passenger door forward, pinning it with his boot to keep it from bouncing back. He cleared his rifle and rolled out of the truck, scrambling for cover behind the rear axle. None of their vehicles offered much in the way of cover, and their best play was to fight through the ambush. Getting everyone turned around and moving back the way they had come wasn't an option.

As soon as Jeff reached the rear of the column, he ran into Wakiel, a tall, sinewy Afghan from the Panshir Valley. They had worked together for years. In broken Dari, Jeff ordered Wakiel to gather his squad for a flanking maneuver. Wakiel chattered into his radio and, within a few moments, the assault squad piled up behind the medical truck, ready to roll.

Jeff didn't remember the Dari word for "flank;" he just stabbed a knife hand up and to the left. His Afghani assaulters knew what to do and they were hot to fight.

The twelve of them, including Jeff, sprinted up the closest ravine, working to gain altitude so they could drop down on the Taliban-infested ridge line. As he pounded up the hill, Jeff could see the Corolla getting mauled in the middle of the bowl. One glance at the car told Jeff he would have men to mourn when the dust settled.

At forty-three years of age, it almost didn't matter how fit Jeff was. Running straight up a mountain in body armor at seven thousand feet made him feel like a lung was going to pop out of his mouth. He had been born with the furthest thing from a "runner's physique." Between his Irish genes and a thousand hours on the weight bench, Jeff could fight eyeball to eyeball with a silver-back gorilla. He had no neck, a foot-thick chest, huge arms, and thighs the size of tree trunks. Like most of the Special Forces operators getting on in age, Jeff didn't mind a bit of a belly bulge sticking over his waistband. His enormous upper body mass and the belly bulge added up to dead weight, though, when running up a mountain in Afghanistan in the middle of a fire fight.

He wasn't about to let Wakiel and his guys get away from him, so Jeff drove harder up the sand and moon dust, his boots filling with gravel and debris, his throat burning like he was sucking on a blow torch. They had been pushing far up a ravine and, as they crested the hill, Jeff could see they were now above the Taliban force.

"Shift fire. Shift fire." Jeff coughed into the radio as his assault team reached the top. Jeff knew his men would plow straight into the Taliban positions without considering that their truck column below, with more than a dozen crew-served machine guns, was pounding that area with everything they had.

"Shift fire, copy?" Jeff heaved for air, trying to gulp down oxygen and listen intently at the same time.

"Roger. Shifting fire up and right," one of the other Green Berets with the column replied, no doubt running up and down the string of trucks trying to get control of sixty adrenaline-crazed Afghani commandos and their belt-fed machine guns.

With his command job done, Jeff launched into the fight himself, hammering rounds from his AK and catching up to his men. They leapfrogged from one piece of cover to the next, driving down on the Taliban positions.

Jeff dove behind a huge boulder and flopped to one side, crabbing around the rock and catching a full view of the battle-field. By climbing high up the hillside, he and his assault team had side-doored the Taliban force and he could see lengthwise into several foxholes filled with enemy. Jeff pushed his AK around the edge of the boulder and dumped rounds into one open foxhole after another, dropping some men to the ground and forcing others to leap out of their trenches and flee into the open. When they did, the truck column in the valley below cut them to pieces.

There was no stopping the carnage now that the smell of blood was in the air. Jeff leapt from behind the boulder, ran forward and fell hard into a hole, stomping a dead man's open guts. The mushy footing caused Jeff to tip and slam into the wall of the ditch. The stench of the man's open bowel hit his face like a slap, making him grimace and turn his head.

The gunfire slowed. Jeff could see four or five surviving Taliban running away over the ridge. The hillside and ridge were littered with bodies. Jeff crawled out of his foxhole and maneuvered over to Wakiel.

"How are the men?" Jeff asked in Dari.

"Is good," Wakiel panted in broken English, coming down from the rush of the last murderous drive.

"*Katar*. Danger," Jeff reminded him. Wakiel nodded.

Jeff had been in hundreds of gunfights and he knew that winning the fight was only the beginning of the work. Policing up the bodies, and figuring out which of them were dead and which were waiting to blow the victors up with a hand grenade, would take hours. There was nothing glamorous about policing a battlefield.

It took three hours for Jeff and his guys to clear the field, and they lined up ten dead Taliban in a row, their AKs, PKMs and RPGs piled beside them. A couple of Jeff's indigenous "*Indij*" guys started taking pictures with their trashy cell phones, holding dead guys up by their hair. They needed the pictures for evidence and to match against the "most wanted" list. Still, the specter made Jeff turn away.

He looked back at his column of trucks. He could see three black body bags lying outside the lead Corolla—the car that had contained his Amniat scouts, some of his best friends and finest warriors. The medics were smoking cigarettes instead of working on his men, which meant Jeff had lost more friends.

Jeff's body felt drained, like a fist unclenching. He would complete this last mission, and then he would leave Afghanistan and warfighting behind forever.

He had been in command of the column of fifteen trucks for three days, and road dust coated his face and the inside of his nose, dragging on every breath. For hours on end, for the last three days, his binoculars had come up and down searching for an ambush, like genuflecting to the gods of war.

Lift the binos. Scan the horizon. Scan big rocks. Scan all potential hiding places. Lower the binos. Check the position of his trucks. Repeat every ninety seconds, forty-five times an hour, five hundred times a day.

From the center of his head to the marrow of his bones, fatigue dogged him. A fighter could only stay hard for so long. For him, it had been twenty-eight years.

Driving for days had worn him down to a nub. The rocking motion of the truck and the chemical body odor from the men commingled with exhaust fumes, kicking his motion sickness into overdrive. Even so, seventy lives depended on him staying rock solid, and now men had died on his watch.

The distance to the Forward Operating Base wasn't the problem. They could have made the drive in ninety minutes going balls out, but the province crawled with Taliban and Jeff's column was anything but low profile: fifteen Toyota Tacomas, painted desert tan, each one of them with a Russian-made belt-fed machine gun bolted to the truck bed.

Jeff had ordered his Amniat scouts in the beat-up Corolla to range out every ten kilometers to reconnoiter the road ahead. Since the scout vehicle looked just like every other piece of junk in this desert, he had hoped the Taliban wouldn't waste bullets on it. Three of Jeff's best *Indij* fighters had been crammed into that little car.

For eight hours, the column had run with two overwatch trucks fanning out to the left and the right, up on the ridge tops, covering the column with their big fifty-caliber belt-fed machine guns. That meant a lot of stop-and-wait inaction as the overwatch trucks maneuvered into new positions. The column would drive a kilometer, wait fifteen minutes for overwatch to set up, then drive a kilometer more. The process yanked on the column like a ball and chain, but it had to be done. Without covering fire, they could find themselves on the death-eating side of an ambush.

War is work, Jeff had been telling himself, manual labor. It wasn't just physically exhausting. It was the waiting that ground the soul down —constant stress and usually nothing to show for it. He knew he was an excellent warfighter, a manual laborer of death and destruction with an iron will. He could control the chaos like few men on earth, and it was this unwavering faith in his own competency that powered Jeff through long and tedious missions like this one.

Now, with the ambush sprung, the battle finished and several of his men dead, Jeff was no longer feeling that same bullet-proof self-confidence.

Wakiel walked over to Jeff, smoking a cigarette.

"I guess that was a bad place to get ahead of our security element," Jeff said in English.

Wakiel knew Jeff well enough to understand and replied, "*Khalash*, Jeff." It was Dari for "finished," but today it meant "farewell."

After this mission, Jeff headed home forever, back to the other world — the world that didn't smell like the inside of an Afghani's lower intestines, the world where he could stay clean, sleep in on a Sunday with his wife, and take in the fresh smell of his sons' hair first thing in the morning.

The sweet-sour smell of shit wafted past his face, and Jeff searched for the offending stench, noticing a green, chunky glob on his boot. With nowhere to wipe it off, Jeff's aggravation peaked, his only solace that he was leaving this endless parade of rot and ruin.

Jeff vowed to never again smell the guts of a man, to never again face the buzz of angry bullets, and to never again watch friends die violent deaths. Back in the *real* world of America, Jeff would put a net around his family and would tie it down tight. The demons of chaos and destruction would forever infest Afghanistan, but they would not follow him home. Whatever affection he had once had for the life of a soldier, it was over. Now he would make damned sure his family lived in peace.

"I am so sick of fighting death every day," Jeff said, looking at his Afghani friend for the last time.

The Afghani barely understood his English, which was the only reason Jeff allowed himself to put words to his fatigue.

Wakiel nodded and returned to smoking his cigarette.

———

Bandar Sharak
    Hormozgan Province, Iran
    Present Day

In the end, Afshin Asadi would explode a dirty bomb over Saudi Arabian soil, not because of his religion or his politics, but because he couldn't stand to leave a project unfinished.

Somewhere in the back of his mind, the same place where he kept information on how to operate his microwave oven, Afshin knew he would go to paradise by sacrificing his life, if it came to that. He accepted the information without any particular interest.

Some might look at Afshin's story and draw the conclusion he had been imprisoned by a cruel government, a regime that would enslave a mentally challenged, but genius young man to an ignorant religion. In their rush to repudiate Islam, they would miss the point.

Truth was, Afshin already lived in paradise, and his government was doing him a favor by confining him to a workshop with a prototype nuclear device. Every morning he awoke with a burning desire to move the project one step closer to completion, and every night he lay down deeply satisfied by the work he had completed. On any given day, he might have tested a candidate polystyrene as a suspension material, or machined a new trial shield panel. Each small step toward completion scratched an itch deep in his soul, and he went to sleep happy as a man could be—at least as a happy as an *autistic* man could be.

Five years previously, as Afshin studied at Amirkabir University of Technology in Tehran, one of his professors had asked him to visit during office hours. When Afshin arrived at the meeting in his professor's office—more a cubbyhole than an office—another man was wedged into a seat in the corner between piles of papers. The strange man wore a crumpled suit coat and a yellowing dress shirt. He was balding and peered over a pair of thick-framed glasses.

The stranger introduced himself, and Afshin failed to note his name, more interested in the big Western-made calculator poking out of the man's shirt pocket. Calculator Man peppered Afshin with engineering and physics questions, beginning with simple ones and moving toward the more complex. Afshin answered plainly, without wondering for a single second about the purpose of the meeting.

More than a month later, the same man interrupted a Thermal Engineering lecture. The teacher's aide pulled Afshin from class and Calculator Man showed him out the front door of the university to a waiting taxi. Afshin never saw the school, nor his family, again.

He might have enjoyed seeing his family but he never requested it. Afshin feared interrupting the work, worried they might pull him off the intensely gratifying process of designing and building an entirely novel type of nuclear weapon. Nobody had ever exploded a dirty bomb before and the technical requirements for the explosive, and the radioactive shielding, ran deep into the speculative.

Afshin's father had served in the Iran-Iraq War, and his mother was a nomadic Iranian exposed to "Yellow Rain" during the war. His mother died of bone cancer, and his father was revered by their town as a war hero, though it only seemed to matter during patriotic holidays.

Afshin had no assistants and almost no supervision. His food and support were provided by government people who appeared occasionally to make sure his tools ran properly and that he was alive and well. When he needed a new end mill or, on the rare occasion when he wanted a pornographic magazine, he placed the order. Nobody bothered him about the pornography, even though it was technically illegal in Iran. The Lebanese porno magazines simply showed up in the bottom of the next box of tooling and raw materials. But the work was almost always more satisfying than the porn, and he took little time off to masturbate.

One day, after five years of laboring over the Russian surplus strontium-90 thermal generator he had been provided as a source for radioactive material, Afshin looked down at his stainless steel workbench and beheld a completed, highly sophisticated dirty bomb. It was no larger than the mini-refrigerator where he kept his sodas, and it weighed just under ninety kilos. The radiation pouring off the casing measured barely more than exposure to the sun in the upper atmosphere.

Two days after completing his bomb, Afshin heard the buzz of a small aircraft taxiing outside. The sounds of small aircraft were commonplace, since his workshop and living quarters were located in an airplane hangar. But this airplane approached his building, which heralded the coming of his boss, Calculator Man.

By now, Afshin knew the professor's name: Ostãd Mumtãz Shahin Nazari. Professor Nazari had visited Afshin many times over the last years, receiving updates on progress and vetting Afshin's data and material requests. Afshin assumed the professor held some rank in the science or military ministry, though Iranian state government interested Afshin about as much as women's perfume which, was to say, not at all.

This visit was different from previous visits. For one thing, the bomb was complete. For another, Professor Nazari appeared to be dying. Afshin didn't ask, but he guessed that cancer was consuming his supervisor. So, for two reasons, Afshin's life was about to change, and that stressed him to distraction.

"*Salaam aleikum,*" The professor greeted him and took his hand. Afshin looked downward in a show of respect.

"*Salaam,* Professor, I am finished." Afshin continued to gaze at the concrete, uncomfortable with looking directly at other peoples' faces.

"Yes, my young friend, you are." The professor released Afshin's hand and shuffled to the work table. "It is beautiful. Allahu Akbar."

Afshin felt his face flush red with pleasure. Indeed, the

device was beautiful and it was gratifying for the professor to say so. Afshin had nothing to say, so he remained silent.

"Are you prepared to test it?" the professor asked, caressing the aluminum casing.

"Yes, Jenaab." Afshin applied the honorific, pleased to have his work acknowledged.

"Afshin, I feel I must tell you, what we are about to do is more than a test. It is a victory for Islam. We shall detonate the device on the Wahabis and their American pipeline. As we kill the pipeline, we kill the link between the Americans and the Saudis, and we force Persia to finally take a stand. Our government has lost the will to act and, like during the war with Iraq, they hold back their love of God, afraid of the West. The Saudis push their Wahabist agenda across the globe, building schools and mosques in every corner of Islam: Afghanistan, Pakistan, Russia, and even America itself. They are the true enemy, but our government refuses to strike. With this bomb, we shall force the ayatollahs to take up the sword Allah has given them. Then the Persian Empire can resume its rightful place. Will you give your life to that cause?"

Afshin understood every word. He was a genius, after all. At the same time, he could care less about religion or the Persian Empire. What he cared about, above all else, was seeing the device tested. He couldn't continue living without seeing the bomb detonate. If he died in the process, that concerned him very little.

"Yes, *Jenaab*," Afshin answered.

"Good, my son. I do consider you my son." The professor smiled. "I must also tell you this. The Guardian Council has not authorized this detonation. We will move forward without approval. My own time is at an end and I am afraid that, without me, our leaders will endlessly dither. We know the righteous path, you and I, and we must act for our country's future. Do you agree, *pesar*?"

"Yes, *Jenaab*," Afshin said for the third time.

"Very well. Please bring the device to my airplane."

Afshin lifted the bomb with a small electric winch hanging from the metal rafters and lowered it onto a pallet truck. They wheeled the bomb out the large door of the hangar, the dying man resting his hand on the younger man's shoulder. The bomb rolled across the tarmac toward the waiting Cessna.

———

Click here to keep reading Black Autumn.

BY JEFF KIRKHAM & JASON ROSS

The Last Air Force One

Black Autumn Travelers

Readyman SmartBook Guides - nonfiction

<u>Premium catalog</u>:

Black Autumn

White Wasteland (releases 9/2019)

More coming soon...

Sign up here to receive your *free* Black Autumn Starter Library, including our interactive bug-out bag checklist.

ABOUT THE AUTHORS

Jeff Kirkham spent almost 29 years as a Green Beret (18ZVW7/W8), with years "boots on the ground" in Afghanistan and Iraq as a member of a counter terrorist direct action unit.

Somehow, he has managed to study 6 foreign languages, earn a Bachelor's of Science, write 3 books (a 4th book is in editing), earn multiple registered patents (one of which is the RATS Tourniquet), and manage his passion project; ReadyMan. Oh, and he's a father of two rambunctious little boys.

The joke around the office is that if a Neanderthal, James Bond, and Q had a baby, it would be Jeff.

Jason Ross has been a hunter, fisherman, shooter and preparedness aficionado since childhood and has spent tens of thousands of hours roughing it in the great American outdoors. He's an accomplished big game hunter, fly fisherman, an Ironman triathlete, SCUBA instructor, and frequent business mentor to U.S. military veterans. He retired from a career in entrepreneurialism at forty-one years of age after founding and selling several successful business ventures.

After being raised by his dad as a metal fabricator, machinist and mechanic, Jason has dedicated twenty years to mastering preparedness tech such as gardening, composting, shooting, small squad tactics, solar power and animal husbandry. Today, Jason splits his time between international humanitarian work, the homeless community and his wife and seven children.

Join the Readyman lifestyle...click the Facebook link below, or find them on their website at http://www.readyman.com and be sure to sign up here for their newsletter to download your free *Black Autumn* Starter Library, and receive updates, news, and new release information.

 facebook.com/ReadyManMedia

The Last Air Force One,
by Jeff Kirkham, Fmr. Army Green Beret
& Jason Ross

Made in the USA
Coppell, TX
05 February 2020

15382964R00097